(Cursed # 1)

By Claire Farrell

First Print Edition

June 2011

Copyright © Claire Farrell 2011

Claire_farrell@live.ie

Book cover images provided by:

© Y0jik @ Dreamstime.com

© Sbelov @ Dreamstime.com

© ApricotBrandy @Dreamstime.com

Licence Notes

Prologue

January

Nathan
Devon, England

One by one, my family members phase into wolves around me. My own wolf paces within the imaginary cage in my mind, waiting impatiently. It's taking me too long to change. They're all watching and wondering what's wrong. Only I know. It's her.

My body aches, but I can't let go of the stress. It's all her fault. I don't know her yet, but she haunts my dreams every night; all of the signs say I'm heading straight for her. She's about to cross my path, and there isn't much I can do about it. Except refuse to love her. Make her hate me.

I hear a snarl and realise it's me. Well, the wolf me. Disagreeing as usual. Relief washes over me as he makes his presence known. He pushes his will against mine and cleanses my thoughts. He wants her. The one he recognises as his true mate.

So I let go. I picture the animal inside escaping and overshadowing my human self. The links entwining both halves break, allowing the wolf to gain centre stage. The floating sensation signals the war between human and animal has been fought and won. Humanity subsides.

Wolf takes over.

A sharp twist of pain and an overpowering rush of adrenalin push me to my knees. I choke a little at the speed of the change. Fingers stretch into claws that sink in the earth, striving for release. My back arches into a curve as a warm coat of coal black fur sprouts from my skin.

My head spins as my face elongates into a snout, and fanged teeth fill my mouth. I shake free of the dizziness, and all of my senses improve immediately. I smell and see everything like the world has been magnified. It's been a year since I first changed, but so much feels brand new to me.

I stretch my new form almost lazily, relishing the sensations that never get old no matter how many times I change. Instinct kicks in, and my body aches to take in every scent around me. My peripheral eyesight transforms. My focus and point of view alter completely.

I am ready.

I am wolf.

Life is less complicated like this. I even catch myself thinking it would be nice to share all of this with her. Humanity recoils at the thought. *Bad idea*, it tells me, but in this form I'm happy. Free.

***

Vin
Bieszczady Mountains, Poland

Far from the snowy peaks of the mountain, surrounded by a dense forest of beech trees, a group of wolves gather together. They are far from the trails the humans like to use. Other animals, even predators, avoid the area once they catch the unique scent of werewolf. Yet still the group remains cautious. Wariness prevails. Rival packs have grouped together in an uneasy truce. The presence of the few lone wolves who skulk the earth without a pack increases the tension. The need to dominate is strong. Instinct urges them to fight, but they wait for news—for the greater good. Edgy and cold, they sit in silence. Numbering less than twenty, they are the last stronghold of their kind.

A silver elder sits alone at the head of the group. He is in no mood for challenges. His mate rests behind him, leaving a considerable amount of distance between them. She snaps a warning at the young male close to her when he tries to inch past. He retreats, his head bowed in a gesture of submission.

The eerie silence is broken only by an occasional low growl. A man appears, red-faced and sweating, his feet scuffing the ground noisily. His presence brings displeasure, but they know him. They know they must tolerate him. At least until he shares the news.

The man's dark brown hair sticks to his forehead as he trembles with fear. The scent entices the wolves to make a move, but they need to hear what he has to say first. The youngest male shivers and growls incessantly, barely able to control himself. He is flanked by two others who nip him to remind him of his manners.

"We've tracked them. Watchers are in place." The man is still panting from the hike. It was never meant to be taken by a human. The wolves are pleased by his words, but many of them sense hesitation in the man's voice.

"There is more. Worse news." A cacophony of growls build up into one single sound. The man tries to back away. He wants no part of this. It makes no difference; they know his weakness. The news will be told regardless.

Many of the wolves phase into their human forms; their nakedness is not their shame.

"What else?" the elder demands.

"They're on the move again. The signs say it's almost time for the pup to mature."

The elder considers the news. "And what of the abomination?"

"No changes, but time is not on our side. She's almost of age."

Some of the wolves growl in unison. A russet coloured wolf moves forward to stand next to the elder. He is joined by two others; one curls back his lip to display a toothy snarl.

The bearer of news can feel the atmosphere change and desperately wants to leave, regretting playing any role in shifter politics. It was a mistake. He can't trust them.

"We have no need for impure females. The girl was always meant to die. As for the pup… take the distraction out of the equation. In the chaos, bring the woman to me."

The man shakes his head. "I can't do that. I'm a seeker; I don't deal with… problems. I can't hurt kids." His voice rises into a desperate whine.

The elder can't help laughing, but he has abandoned his human side for so long that it sounds like an odd bark.

"I wasn't talking to you." With an unspoken signal, a trio of wolves advance on the man.

Along the summit of the Bieszczady Mountains, a group of howling wolves draw little attention.

Chapter One

February

Perdita
Dublin, Ireland

"Oh, for God's sake. I'll wear the bloody jumper. Just shut up already!"

I had finally snapped. I couldn't help it.

"You will not!" shrieked my grandmother at the exact same time as my father shouted at me to stop swearing.

I sighed wearily, resting my head in my hands, preparing myself to sit there until they finished rowing. They ignored me and launched back into each other almost straight away. Typical.

"I won't have it any more, Stephen. I mean it! You can't tell her what to wear. You've no right."

"I'm her father. I have every right. I don't want her wandering the streets like a tart. If she wants to be seen outside then she can cover herself up."

"A tart? Do you hear yourself? You must be the only man in Ireland who wants his sixteen-year-old daughter to look like a boy. A tart... because she wants to wear clothes her own mother bought her. The nerve of you!"

The constant arguments were slowly driving me insane. I jumped up, emboldened by anger, and walked straight over to the front door.

"Where do you think you're going?" My Dad's eyes widened in disbelief.

"Out. To Tammie's house."

"You're not going out at this time of night, Perdy," he said, his voice firm and resolute, never expecting an argument.

I gave him a withering look reserved for very important occasions.

"Dad, it's not even six o'clock. That's not night. It's not exactly pitch black outside. I'm tired of this. You two can argue all you like; I'm not listening to it anymore. When you both grow up and sort yourselves out, then let me know. This has *never* been about me."

I glared at the two of them, watching their faces reddening with shame because they knew I was right. Their battles were a front for the bitterness they couldn't discuss. They didn't try to stop me leaving, much to my relief. It would have been mortifying if my rebellion was overturned before I actually left the house. I shrugged on my denim jacket and picked up the jumper but made a point of carrying it out the door.

Outside, I took a deep relaxing breath. Exhaling slowly, I felt a lot calmer as I made my way over to Tammie Rutherford's house. My best friend would absolutely understand if I hid in her house for a few hours. She knew better than anyone how much I needed a break from Dad and Gran. Sometimes they were toxic together.

Tonight's row had been about clothes, as per usual. My mother's idea of parenting was to either send me business newsletter type emails about her life or clothes guaranteed to launch Gran and Dad into a miniature war.

The battles were constant because they never agreed with each other. They both wanted me to do things their way. Neither of them seemed to care about what I wanted.

I loved my Dad, but I didn't get him. He was so busy trying to protect me from the world that he kept forgetting to let me live in it. I didn't want to hide away because of a few hypothetical what ifs.

I loved my Gran, but I hated the way she encouraged me to break the rules, because it was me who had to deal with the aggro over it. She was flamboyant and liked to be noticed; I could never be that person, no matter how much she tried to force it on me.

Tammie didn't live far from me, so I was there within minutes. That was long enough to mull things over and calm down a little. Tammie was the youngest of six; her family were really loud and relaxed about everything. I knocked at her door, beginning to feel a little embarrassed that I had walked out of my house in a temper. Her Dad answered, his eyebrows rising in surprise when he saw me.

"Perdy? Does your Dad know you're here?"

"Yeah," I said, feeling irrationally grumpy that everyone in the world seemed to know my Dad's rules almost as well as I did. "Tammie here?"

"I think so." He looked puzzled for a few seconds; he regularly had trouble keeping track of who was at home. It was the sort of thing that drove my Dad crazy. He could never rely on Tammie's father to know if I was in his house or not.

"Tammie! You here?" Tammie's Dad shouted, making me jump.

I heard a few bangs before Tammie ran down the stairs, stopping abruptly when she saw me.

"Hey," she said, sounding surprised. "Dad, get lost." He wandered back in, good-naturedly patting her on the head as he passed her by.

"What's going on Per?"

I shrugged. "Walked out. Two of them at each other again, driving me insane."

She nodded. "Come on in. We've the room to ourselves for a bit." I followed her upstairs to the bedroom she shared with one of her older sisters. It was small and messy, but at least it looked lived in. Unlike mine. She shook a bottle of electric blue nail varnish violently, and then settled down to paint her toenails.

"Right, what happened then?"

I lay back on her bed, feeling frustrated. My life just wasn't my own. Dad couldn't let me do anything, and Gran kept trying to use me to make him mad. I didn't say any of that though.

"Remember that purple blouse thing my mother sent me a few weeks ago? Well, Gran pretty much made me wear it when we went food shopping earlier. Dad happened to drive past us on his way home from work, saw the top, and flipped his lid. He was at home waiting for us and went off on one about wearing a stupid jumper over tarty clothes if I was out in public. That just kicked everything off."

Tammie sniggered. "He thinks that blouse is tarty? I should send you home in one of *my* outfits."

I groaned. "He'd lock me in the attic or something. Seriously, Tams, he's getting worse. I said I was going out, and he was all, you can't go out at this time of night, blah, blah, blah. It's still day time!"

"What the hell is he afraid of? That you might actually get a life? No offence, Perdy, but he might as well have you locked in the attic. It's not like you go anywhere anyway. You're not even allowed sleep over here." She made a face at that injustice. She had stopped inviting me long ago.

"It's not my fault, Tammie; it's not worth the hassle. None of this is. I'm so tired of it though. I just want... I don't know what I want. Something to happen. Something to change. I'm so bored of everything."

"You could ask your Mam can you stay with her for a while."

"Eh, yeah. Doubt that would happen," I replied, wondering why she couldn't get it into her head that my mother just wasn't interested in me.

"Ah, I don't know then. You could always stay here."

I smiled at her. It was nice of her to offer, but her house was already full to the brim. Besides, I couldn't handle the noise for too long. I was too used to being alone. Gran was officially supposed to babysit me whenever Dad worked, but she pretty much snuck off most of the time to her Senior Citizen nights. She always said she was off to play bowls, but anytime she called me, I would hear pub noise in the background. As if a sixteen year old needed a babysitter anyway.

I stayed in Tammie's house until it got late. I didn't want to go home, so I let her test out makeup on me, because I knew she liked that. When Dad arrived to pick me up, I didn't make a fuss. He raised his eyebrow when he spotted the sparkly green eye shadow but, to his credit, didn't mention it.

In fact, he didn't say a thing on the way home. He sat in the kitchen and fidgeted while Gran made a pot of tea.

They glanced at each other before Gran began to speak.

"Perdy, we're really sorry about earlier. You were right. We do need to... sort ourselves out."

Dad nodded in agreement. "I don't want you to feel badly about us rowing, so we've agreed to make more of an effort. It won't happen again."

I glared at them, irritated by their attempts to brush things under the carpet. "What won't happen again? She won't want me to do one thing while you want the opposite of me? Things have to change around here or... or I'm not staying."

Gran's hand flew to her mouth; Dad's face drained of colour. For once, they both looked like they were on the same page.

"What?" I said.

"What do you want from us?" Dad said. His voice shook, and that scared me a little, but I figured I had to take my chances wherever they came.

"Look. I'm almost seventeen. I don't need anyone telling me what to wear. I don't need a babysitter. I don't need you two arguing over every single part of my life. I've never gotten into trouble, so I think I should be allowed some freedom. I think I should be allowed to do things that other teenagers do. I think I've earned your trust by now, Dad. If I mess up, then punish me. But don't punish me for things I haven't done yet. And Gran, you need to stop using me to prove points to Dad. It's not fair on me."

I took a deep breath and glanced at them both to see how they were taking it. I couldn't believe I had the guts to say all that. I usually went along with everything they said, but I needed to start standing up for myself.

They both looked a little winded. The silence only frustrated me further.

"Fine. I'm going to bed," I said. "And I'm getting the bus to school with Tammie from now on."

I hurried up the stairs to my room before either of them could argue with me. Locking the door behind me, something I knew would infuriate my Dad, I sat on my bed and texted Tammie with an update. I made a decision about my own life, and I was going to stick by it. I just hoped I had the guts to go through with it.

The high from winning a small battle left me too quickly. I suddenly felt deflated, worried, and even a little scared. I had done some things I never had before: answered back, told Dad and Gran what I wanted, hadn't bothered listening to their arguments. Yet the world hadn't ended. Tammie once said to me, "What's the worst that could happen?" And so far, she had been right. Nothing bad had come from me standing up for myself. *Better do it more often*, I thought, yawning loudly.

I checked my email, automatically deleting an unread one from my mother, before deciding I was too tired to stay awake. I barely managed to comb out my hair before my eyes began to close by themselves. I lay down, praying I would have that dream again. For months, I had been dreaming about a boy. At least, I thought that's what they were about. The dreams themselves were out of focus, confusing and vague, but the main point was me reaching something. Someone. Someone with beautiful brown eyes that made my insides melt.

I knew it was a dream, but it felt as though it was leading me somewhere. Waking up from such a dream left me with a warm feeling inside, yet the way it ended was always frustrating. I hadn't gotten to where I was supposed to be. It left a sense of longing inside me that I couldn't get rid of. I didn't know what a recurring dream signified, but this one made me feel as if I always woke before the most important part. It was like having a word on the tip of your tongue for a year, or being on the verge of remembering something you were supposed to do, but not quite getting there.

I forgot about everything except those eyes as I relaxed into a deep sleep, still hoping for a good dream. I wasn't disappointed. Wind whipped my hair backward as I sped through a forest. I must have been flying because my feet didn't touch the ground. Not flying exactly. Gliding. It was dark, but I wasn't scared. I knew I was meant to be there. I was looking for something. Something was waiting for me.

An orb of light danced ahead of me, leading my way. It soon paused and changed direction, finally guiding me along a path to an ancient oak tree that towered above.

I looked around, awestruck, until I noticed a figure under the tree. The dream blurred; the atmosphere turned cold. I could tell their back was to me, so I reached out. There was something bad nearby. I could sense it. I had to warn them. As my fingers touched the skin on the back of their neck, a thrilling jolt of electricity ran up my arm. I laughed out loud; this was all the way it was supposed to be. The figure whirled around, momentarily scaring me with a flash of something sharp and white, but then my gaze locked onto the most beautiful pair of eyes I had ever seen. Eyes so familiar to me. My fears melted away, and everything else dimmed.

Chapter Two

I was torn from my dream by the jarring sound of my alarm clock. Turning it off, I indulged in an extra few minutes in bed, trying my hardest to remember every second of my dream. As usual it made no sense to me, but something about it calmed me, made me happy. All too soon my good mood was lost to the memory of the night before. I had to face Dad and Gran, but worse, I had to pick an outfit that wouldn't annoy either of them. I decided to wear my dressing gown to breakfast and then figure out what to do next based on how they acted. Relieved to have some sort of a plan, I wandered downstairs. They were both up already and had even made breakfast for me.

I sat down warily with the strangest sensation that this was the calm before the storm. Both of them were exceptionally polite to each other and me. It was a little too pod people for my liking.

"So?" I said, eventually. "Are we going to talk about it?" I hated when they dragged things out.

Dad folded his newspaper with slow, careful moments. Gran took a long sip of her morning coffee. Obviously neither of them wanted to start. I began to feel as though I was the parent, and they were the kids. Finally, after a few pointed looks from me, Dad cleared his throat.

"We had a long talk last night. Everything you said was pretty reasonable, so I'm prepared to make some changes. But if you let me down…."

"We don't want you to feel like you have to leave us to be happy," Gran said. "We all need to get out of the past. We were thinking that maybe we could make a fresh start, you know? We could redecorate together. You could do your room the way you want."

"And you can pick your own clothes. Within reason," Dad said. "Maybe stay out a bit later at weekends. We'll see."

They looked innocent enough, but I couldn't help feeling suspicious. Gran was anal about keeping our house the way it had been when my mother lived there, and my Dad was anal about letting me do anything normal. I didn't really trust either of them to stick to their word. It would be interesting to see what happened next.

"Okay," I said. "We'll see all right."

I finished my breakfast and ran back upstairs to get ready. I pulled my hair back into a tight plait and turned my attention to clothes. That was the thing. I hated my Dad telling me what I couldn't wear, but the truth was that I had never had the confidence to wear the kinds of clothes he hated anyway. I quite liked feeling hidden under the heavy jumpers he preferred me.

I ended up throwing on a pair of jeans and a thick black cardigan. I buttoned it all the way, hiding the bright coloured shirt underneath. Feeling a little daring, I even put on some clear lip gloss and the tiniest smudge of eyeliner. Satisfied, I got my things together, put on my jacket, and raced down stairs to meet Tammie on time.

"You sure you don't want a lift?" Dad asked, his tone hopeful.

"I'm sure."

"Maybe you'd like to wear your hair down today. It's so pretty down," Gran said, looking wistful.

"No, Gran," I said as firmly as I could. Surprisingly enough, they both left me alone after that. Cheering up, I waved goodbye and left on time. Thinking, *so far, so good*. I stood at the end of my road and waited patiently for Tammie. She texted me to see if I was really there and then turned up a few minutes later.

"Hi," she said with an excited squeal. "You're free!"

I couldn't help laughing. "Maybe. Baby steps right now."

We walked toward the bus stop slower than I liked because Tammie couldn't walk in her heels. She wore a short denim skirt and ankle boots with stiletto heels. I wasn't even the slightest bit surprised when I noticed her shudder violently. Early spring in Ireland meant it would be pretty cold for a while, so I was glad of the heavy cardigan and the extra padding from the denim jacket. The sun hadn't fully risen yet. The darkness of the winter months seemed to linger on for as long as possible. A sharp nip in the wind and that distinct cold smell in the air made it feel like winter, but it was good to be outside. I was happier than I should have been on such a dull morning.

Tammie began to sing loudly, inducing an eye roll from me. I might have stayed under the radar, but she liked to be noticed. The more popular girls hated her and did their best to make her feel bad about herself, but she never listened.

When the bus finally arrived, we sat in the middle seats by the heater so Tammie could defrost her legs. I heard a couple of insulting comments about Tammie's appearance from the back seat, but she wasn't in the least bit bothered by it.

When she had warmed herself, she perked up long enough to share a titbit of gossip with me. "I heard a rumour a family moved into one of those big old houses near the woods. Maybe there'll be someone new at school."

I shrugged, not particularly interested. There were a lot of empty houses around. We lived too far on the outskirts of the city to attract many new families, chiefly because visiting anywhere useful meant travelling by bus or car.

This particular group of houses had gotten run down because they remained empty for so long with no upkeep. The small wooded area was dense enough for lots of alcohol drinking teenagers to hide in at the weekends. Tammie and I were never invited. Not that I would have been allowed out that late anyway.

The local gossip out of the way, it was time to talk about my cousin, Joey. Aside from Tammie, Joey was my only other friend at school. Tammie had a major long-term crush on him, which was probably the reason we started hanging around with him in the first place. We made an odd trio. He was the brainy nerd, she was the kooky outsider, and I was, well, I was a bit of a non-entity. I was invisible. Joey had no idea that Tammie liked him. This was handy for me; there was no telling how weird things could become if my only friends began a relationship together.

We met up with Joey outside school, but he was too busy obsessing over his history homework to have an actual conversation with us. Tammie and I gossiped until the bell rang for our first class. The three of us walked there together, but while Joey sat right up front, Tammie and I sat further down the back. Even a major crush couldn't persuade Tammie to sit up front.

I often wondered what Tammie saw in Joey. He wasn't all that good looking, and they had nothing in common. He looked a lot like my Dad, he was a good four inches shorter than Tammie, and he was a little bit scrawny to boot. He already had his books out and was busy looking very studious.

Tammie was pretty outspoken and wasn't interested in the academic side of things at all. A member of a primarily adult drama club, she spent a good portion of her school time trying to persuade teachers that we needed a drama club at school too. Joey didn't believe in doing things like that when he could be studying.

The teacher came into the room and immediately began to read from the history book. Almost instantly, everyone stopped paying attention. Apart from Joey. Our history teacher had the most boring voice in the world and no teaching skills to speak of. Every single class, he read aloud in a monotonous tone. Yeah, fascinating. Double history on a Monday morning was a punishment from God.

Stifling a yawn, I noticed some of the girls gesture mockingly toward Tammie. Today's joke being her hair. Short and blonde, she had fashioned it into a wild looking spiky style that was tipped with hot pink.

One girl in particular, Dawn Talbot, took on the evil cheerleader persona of American high school films with relish. She regularly gave Tammie a particularly hard time. Even as I glanced around the room, I spotted her sneering at Tammie and whispering things that sent her group of friends into fits of giggles. She was very popular and very mean, and I had yet to figure out how the two were linked. She caught my disapproving eye and threw me a scornful look. I quickly bent my head before she could start an argument. I was always ready to stick up for Tammie, but confrontation on my own behalf didn't come quite as easily.

I sighed to myself before resuming my regular time-wasting activity of scribbling on my books. I was okay at art, and I tended to sketch a lot in my spare time. It helped me relax. Even when I found myself drawing a pair of familiar looking eyes on the inside cover of my history book. Half of my schoolwork was decorated by those dream eyes. I had spent way too much time daydreaming about them. Frustratingly, I could see them clearly in my head, but I still hadn't managed to reproduce them on paper accurately. It gave me a little ache inside that I would never tell Tammie about. Not that I had ever told her about my dreams either. Some things, even your best friend wouldn't understand.

Glancing up at the clock above the whiteboard, I groaned as I realised just how much time was left before the next class. Tammie gave me a sympathetic smile before sneaking her phone out of her bag to read her text messages.

Most of the rest of the class were slouched back in their chairs, passing notes or sending silent texts. Aaron Hannigan entertained himself by throwing pieces of wet paper at the less popular kid in front of him, much to the amusement of the easily pleased girl sitting next to him. Dawn Talbot's shoulder-length blonde hair was being brushed by one of her clones, and Abbi Mitchell decided to irritate everyone around her by filing her nails noisily.

Bored of people watching, I bent my head and continued drawing on my book. I was vaguely aware that the classroom door had opened and that most of the girls in the room had started whispering loudly, but I was too busy carefully filling in an iris to look up. What interested them rarely interested me.

"Students, this is Nathan Evans, the newest pupil to join your class. I trust you'll all welcome him. Now sit down the back there, lad," the most boring teacher in the world said.

The new kid passed through the room amidst excited whispers. In the middle of double history, almost anything becomes something to discuss. But Tammie kept kicking me under the table as hard as she could, hinting at me to look up.

I frowned at her. Rolled my eyes as she nudged me urgently. Glanced up just as Nathan Evans was about to pass by my table. We looked right at each other, and my mouth gaped open in shock. He paused, looking as startled as I felt. I knew him. Or at least, I knew his eyes. I had just drawn them in my book. The hairs rose on the back of my neck as a shiver of excitement ran through me. How was this possible? How could I have seen his eyes in my dreams? The hint of surprise on his face quickly turned into a deep frown that brought me back to earth. My cheeks flushed with heat, and I quickly looked down at my book.

He moved on and sat in an empty seat at the back of the room, but I could have sworn I still felt his eyes burning into me. I groaned inwardly. *Why did I have to freak out the new kid by staring in his face like that?* Most of the class were still nudging each other and whispering, but my hands trembled so much I didn't trust myself to pick up my pen. Never mind look into their faces to see if they were talking about me or him.

"Perdy, are you okay? What on earth was that about?" Tammie hissed in my ear.

I shrugged, trying to come across as nonchalant. I had the strongest urge to turn around in my seat and stare at him again to see how alike those eyes really were. That compulsion scared me enough to make me want to run out of the classroom and never return. There were some things you couldn't live down. I learned that the hard way as I heard Dawn loudly remark, "Isn't it sweet that the freak has a crush on the new boy?" Most people giggled, especially because my face had probably turned tomato red. Tammie stuck her middle finger up at Dawn in response. I cringed and kept my head down for the rest of the class.

I couldn't stop thinking about him. It was as though that word had finally launched itself off the tip of my tongue. Big-time relief, as though something I had been waiting a long time for had finally arrived. I knew it made no sense, but a sneaky thought kept popping into my head. His look had echoed my own. He recognised me, too.

As soon as the bell rang, I picked up my things and ran out of the room, making sure I was the first one to leave. I hurried to the science lab alone to avoid Tammie's questions. Most of the people who passed me by pushed against me roughly as if I didn't exist. I kept my head down, avoided eye contact and made it to the class first as usual.

Except, I wasn't actually first. I only realised this when I walked straight into the new kid who was already casually standing outside the locked door. I gazed at him in confusion, wondering how he had gotten there so quickly, before getting my act together and moving to the other side of the door.

I stole a quick glimpse, but he caught me so I looked away before I could get drawn in and embarrass myself again. I closed my eyes in a sort of despair as it occurred to me that he probably thought I was stalking him or something.

Luckily, it wasn't long before the rest of our classmates joined us and surrounded him, bombarding him with questions and giving me plenty of opportunities to sneak glances at him. He was quite good looking once I got past his eyes. In class, a lot of girls argued over who got to sit next to him.

Even though plenty of girls obviously liked him already, he didn't seem cocky or arrogant. He chatted back to anyone who spoke to him, so he was pretty friendly. I had never really had a type, but he made the butterflies in my stomach flutter extra fast.

His skin was nice and clear, the colour of milky coffee. Dimples chased his smile, which was sort of adorable. His hair was jet black, straight, and cut in a way that wasn't particularly fashionable, but it suited him. He was better looking than any of the other boys in my year, but again, it was his eyes that called to me. It was remarkable how similar they were to the ones in my dream. Big, very dark brown ones that lit up when he smiled. There was something sincere and nice about his entire face. In short, he was hot. Way too hot for me to keep looking at.

But look I did. I couldn't help myself. I found myself peeking at him all day. I caught his eye more than once. Every time he looked at me, I felt as though he knew what I was thinking. There was something really intense about him, and I couldn't understand how everyone else was so easy in his company. I could feel myself crumbling if he merely glanced at me.

I saw him everywhere I went as he was in so many of my classes. Even when he was surrounded by people, I still knew exactly where he was, but I didn't have the guts to start a conversation with him. Knowing me, my mouth would dry up, I'd stutter something nonsensical, and probably trip and fall into a bin for good measure.

Lunchtime was a quick relief because I couldn't spot him in the canteen, and I had some company in the shape of Tammie and Joey. I waited until Joey took a really big bite out of his roll before I talked to him about Dad and Gran.

"I walked out of my house last night, Joe."

He choked on a piece of bread, spluttering for a few minutes before swallowing noisily.

"What do you mean, walked out?"

"They were fighting again, so I left and went to Tammie's house." I tried not to laugh at the gormless look on his face.

"What did they say?" He knew quite well what things were like for me, although he agreed with some of it, like wearing heavy navy jumpers and avoiding boys. Tammie was a bit of a feminist, and it disturbed her greatly that she was attracted to an old-fashioned chauvinist who thought my Dad's rules were for my own good because I was 'just' a girl.

"Gran offered to let me paint my room however I like, and Dad said I could wear what I wanted, pretty much. And that I could maybe stay out later and do some stuff. As long as I don't mess up."

"But why did they take you seriously? You always moan about their rows. It's never stopped them before," he said.

I shrugged; I hadn't thought of that. "I don't know. I got really angry with them and told them I'd leave if they didn't cop on."

"Wow." He took another bite of his roll, and then spoke with his mouth full.

"You must have really scared them."

"What do you mean?"

"You know. Hinting you'd go to your Mam's," he said. "That would kill them both."

"Oh," I said slowly as comprehension dawned on me. I hadn't meant I'd leave for her house. I hadn't even really meant that I would actually leave, but of course, that was their worst nightmare. I had accidentally touched a nerve. I didn't get why they would ever believe I might want to spend time with my mother, but they rarely made sense to me.

"She's a bit slow sometimes, isn't she?" Tammie said. "Anyway, it's up to us to make sure that she doesn't get into any trouble, or she'll be right back where she started. Having no life at all."

I stuck my tongue out at Tammie, but she was right, I would have even less privileges if it all went wrong.

Joey looked thoughtful. "I suppose I better keep an eye out, just in case any of the tossers around here start sniffing around." He glared around the room as if trying to figure out who needed to be watched the most.

Tammie and I exchanged eye rolls. For some reason, Joey seemed to think that the entire male population of the town left Tammie and me alone because of his presence only.

"Okay, who's up for a walk to the shop? I'm in desperate need of a Snickers." Tammie stood and picked up her bag.

I made a face. "Eh, it's raining. No chance."

"I'll go," Joey volunteered. "Wouldn't mind one myself."

They left together, Tammie throwing me a sneaky wink as she walked away. Their need for a snack might be worth facing the now steady rain outside, but there was no way I was willingly going to let my hair get wet over a bar of chocolate. Besides, I got the feeling that Tammie wanted to be alone with Joey. I had homework to get through while she tried to… whatever.

I attempted to concentrate on my French homework, but without Tammie and Joey's chatter, I was hopelessly distracted by thoughts of the new boy, Nathan. I glanced around the room as I tried in vain to memorise a list of verbs and noticed a girl I had never seen before walking across the canteen while struggling to carry a mountain of books. I didn't know her, so she had to be new.

She looked very young and innocent. Sort of like a pretty little china doll. Her hair was dark and wavy, and as she turned her head I saw it reached her waist. She wore a long, vibrantly coloured gypsy style skirt and noisy bangles on her wrists.

Out of the corner of my eye, I saw Dawn and her friends pointing in the girl's direction. I instantly knew they would hassle her. For some reason, my hackles went up. I felt strangely protective of the kid. She was all alone and dressed differently to Dawn and her crowd, which made her a prime target.

The group of girls strode arrogantly toward her—predators confident of the power they held over their prey. They surrounded her, doing their best to intimidate her as they giggled together. She looked so uncertain that I felt a pang of pity for her. Before I had time to even think about it, I was already standing up.

Abbi pushed roughly against the girl's shoulder while Dawn swung her bag toward the pile of books the girl carried. The new girl lost her balance from the impact and fell backward as all of the books slipped out of her hands. Dawn and her cackling friends moved on. I was already hurrying over when Dawn glanced back over her shoulder to admire her work.

"Whoops, so sorry," she said, her voice dripping with sarcasm.

How dare they? I forgot about hiding away in my outrage.

"Oi!" I shouted at the girls, a little too loudly. People started to look in our direction. "What the hell do you think you're doing?"

The girls turned and just stared at me in disbelief. Dawn's eyebrow lifted as she looked me up and down.

"Excuse me?" she said.

"Something wrong with your hearing?" I snapped back. Everyone in earshot laughed as Dawn's face turned from red to purple. The laughter was mostly down to my unusual reaction. Everybody loved seeing someone lose the plot. For once, I didn't even care.

"So, what is it then? Do you lot feel all big and brave when you pick on someone? Safety in numbers and all that. *One* girl, who's obviously younger than you all, isn't going to do much against six of you, is she? That how you get your kicks? Pathetic. Sad pack of sheep," I said, wanting to throw something.

Dawn laughed without humour. "As if I care what a freak like you thinks!"

"I'd rather be a freak than have to put other people down to feel good about myself." I turned to the new girl and helped her up before picking up some of her books.

"You okay? Don't pay any attention to the Queen Bee and her drones over there. This is the best it's going to get for them, so they have to make the most of it the only way they know how. By acting like spineless little bitches. You should be flattered that they don't expect you to be just like them, actually."

I suddenly realised that a lot of people had gathered around us to listen. I lost my nerve and shut up, but it was too late, people were already clapping. A lot of them had been Dawn's targets in the past. Dawn looked horrified, but she bit her lip and let her friends lead her out of the canteen. Some of them had the decency to look ashamed, but they still didn't stand up to her or apologise to the new girl.

The crowd wandered away once they realised the mini drama was over, leaving me and the girl in the centre of the canteen. She grinned at me in such a friendly way that I couldn't help grinning back. I was a little startled to see that her eyes looked familiar, too. I really needed to get over the eye obsession. I carried on picking up the girl's books before putting them on one of the tables so I could shake the hand she extended.

"Thanks for the help," she said. "I'm Amelia. I just started here."

I couldn't place her accent, but it definitely wasn't Irish. I didn't want to throw a load of questions at her if she was only new.

"Hey Amelia, I'm Perdita... but everyone calls me Perdy, unfortunately."

She smiled at me broadly, making me feel totally at ease, which was a rarity for me.

"Pretty name," she said.

I shrugged. "What's your next class? I'll walk you and help carry your books. We should probably find your locker first so you can ditch some of them though."

"Oh, right. I've P.E. next, so I need to head to the gym hall, but my locker is on the way," she said. "I started school today, so I'm a bit lost. Thanks again for the help. I was beginning to think that nobody could pass for friendly in this place."

I gathered up my own things; we divided her pile between us, and then headed toward her locker. "Those girls were just bored. They're like that with all of us, so don't take it personally. I'm pretty sure they'll leave you alone now though."

"Yeah, maybe," she said, sounding unconvinced. She looked shaken, and I didn't get the impression she was used to that sort of treatment.

"So, do you live nearby?" she asked.

I nodded. "Yep. With my Dad and Gran. My Dad works in the hospital."

"He's a doctor?"

I nodded. "Anyway, not much goes on around here. We're only living here 'cos we stay with my Gran, and my Dad's job is nearby. Just waiting until college, and then I'm outta here."

She laughed. "I'm sure it isn't that bad. I'm not really used to anything special anyway."

We dumped most of her books in her locker. I decided to walk her to the P.E. hall just in case Dawn tried to make trouble for her. She still seemed really shy, so I felt as though I should be more welcoming.

"Um, so… if you need any help with anything else, just ask. And hey, if you're not busy tomorrow, you could always join me and my friends at lunch. There's only the three of us, so if you have other plans don't worry about it." I added the last sentence hurriedly and managed to make myself sound lonely *and* desperate. But she thanked me, smiling, and we swapped mobile numbers.

I left her at the gym, promising to see her the next day, and hurried off to my own class which I was now late to. I still had a smile on my face from chatting to Amelia when I realised Nathan was standing in my way. Even though I knew that, logically, he wasn't the boy from my dream, I still felt jumpy when I saw him. My stomach flipped whenever I looked at him. Dream eyes or not.

I moved to walk around him, but he sort of put out his arm to block me. At least, that's what it looked like.

"Hi," he said, so low I could barely hear him. He stared at me in a way I didn't understand. As his eyes searched mine, my cheeks grew hot and, predictably, my mouth dried up. Lo and behold, my brain turned to mush. I mumbled something back at him and scurried past, cursing my social awkwardness. I couldn't function normally in his presence at all.

By the time school ended, it was raining quite heavily, so I was relieved to see my Aunt Stella's car outside. She was always up for giving Tammie and me a lift home, especially in bad weather. Her pet dog, Dolly, took up most of the back seat, but the dog's head was out of the window, panting heavily. I saw lots of people avoiding the car in case she jumped out. She wasn't dangerous, but her size made her look intimidating. Moreover, she drooled a lot. People tended to avoid dog drool.

She whined softly in anticipation when she noticed me and practically squeezed half her body out of the window to get to me. I shoved her back in, with difficulty, before joining her in the back. Stella turned around to talk to me, but Dolly flipped out. She launched herself at the window, almost squashing me in the process. The hackles on the back of her neck were raised as she gave a low warning growl. Hushing her, I glanced out the window, but all I saw was Nathan standing a few yards away looking at the car. Dolly sat back down but kept her front paw on my leg protectively.

"That was weird," I said to Stella who nodded in agreement. I looked back out at Nathan, but he was gone. I wasn't sure if Dolly had been growling at him, or if he had stopped walking because of the noise she was making. Tammie and Joey got into the car so Stella started the engine and set off. Dolly had calmed down, but she was still acting strange. She wouldn't move away from me for even a second, so I felt as if I was stuck in a corner.

When I got home, Dad and Gran were both around and making a show of being nice to each other. I couldn't concentrate on them because I was too busy thinking about Nathan and how many times he had caught me looking at him throughout the day. I pushed my dinner around my plate distractedly as they tried to prove they liked each other and could get along. I ended up going to bed early just so I could think in peace. Before I fell asleep, I realised I had only heard Nathan say one word, but I had spent the entire day obsessing over him. That was crazy. Even for me.

That night I had one of my recurring dreams again. This time the eyes came with a distinguishable face. Nathan's. In my dream, I had the overwhelming sense that he was *mine*. He belonged to me. I sat up straight in the darkness, sweat dripping down my back, completely unnerved all over again. I wasn't sure if my dream had changed because I had spent so much time thinking about him or not. Either way, those dreams were affecting every part of my life. It took me a long time to fall back asleep that night.

Chapter Three

The next morning, I met up with Tammie at the bus stop. Another cold day. It had rained throughout the night.

Tammie was far too hyper for my liking. I wasn't a morning person at the best of times. I hadn't had enough sleep the night before between waking up from strange dreams and then tossing and turning while worrying about said dreams.

"So how were the odd couple last night?" Tammie danced on the spot to keep warm. I mentally prepared myself to hide if anyone saw her.

"Fine, I suppose. Pretending to get along. Long may it last."

"They could be worse," she said.

"How?"

"I dunno. Just could be."

"Whatever." I rolled my eyes. I knew for a fact Tammie would go insane if she had to live by my Dad's rules. "Oh!" I said, remembering something I was supposed to tell her. "I invited a new girl to sit with us at lunch today."

Tammie raised her eyebrows. Maybe because she knew I couldn't string a sentence together in front of someone I don't know.

"Come on, Tams. Give her a chance. She's younger than us, and she got hassled by Dawn and her crowd, so I said she could sit with us. She's nice though. I promise. Her name's Amelia."

"Hmm, we'll see," she said, before grinning mischievously. "Speaking of nice, did you see the fine specimen of a teenage boy who joined history yesterday? Yummy. Oh, wait, silly me, of course you saw him. Your bloody jaw dropped when he walked in. What was that about?"

I blushed. "That's not what happened. Don't be ridiculous."

"Oh, please," she scoffed. "For once I agree with Dawn. It was only obvious you liked him. Bit of a relief that you finally noticed a boy actually. I was starting to think you must fancy *me*."

"Oh, whatever. *Joey!*"

"Cheap shot, Perdy." It was her turn to blush.

The bus rattled up the road before she could think of anything else to embarrass me with. We sat in our usual seats, ignoring the filthy looks Dawn threw our way. The windows were so full of condensation that I couldn't see a thing outside.

We had been on the bus for a few stops when I was surprised to hear somebody call my name. Amelia sat down on the double seat facing us. I tried to say hello but stuttered to a stop when Nathan sat down next to her. I looked at Tammie in confusion, but she was too busy giving Nathan an appreciative glance to notice.

He smiled at us, his knee tipping off mine, and I froze. *Oh, crap.* Those few seconds felt like eternity as I had a mini panic attack in my head, not knowing what to say. Dawn saved me, sort of, by calling to Nathan very loudly in an incredibly snobby tone of voice—even for her.

"Nathan! We're all sitting back here. There's a space right by me, so you don't have to sit next to *them*." She spat out the word *them* as if we were rotting with some contagious disease. The implication was clear. We were not worth sitting next to or near, and we weren't the type of people he should mix with unless he wanted to catch the outcast gene.

I was a little annoyed on behalf of Tammie and Amelia and even thought about answering Dawn back, but Nathan got in there first.

"No, thanks. I'd rather sit here next to my sister. You know, one of *them*. I'd introduce you, but I think you've already met," he called back, even louder than Dawn.

Dawn blushed furiously, slumping low in her seat as if it would hide her away. An eerie silence filled the bus—only broken when Tammie burst into husky laughter. I gazed at Amelia and Nathan, marking the similarities. Now they were both in front of me, I could see the resemblance.

They had different colours and textures to their hair, different builds and skin colour, but their features were alike after all. His accent was pretty similar to hers too, I just hadn't heard him say enough words to notice before. I couldn't stop looking at him—again—as he glared at Dawn, but I realised his eyes weren't angry. In fact, they twinkled with amusement.

He caught my eye and winked. I bit my lip and looked away, anything to be able to speak again. I knew I had to be the one who started the introductions.

"Well, um, this is Amelia… Amelia, this is my best friend Tammie… and erm, that girl at the back of the bus kicking herself is Dawn."

They all laughed, shattering the tension.

"Ah, yes, I recognise Dawnie Dearest now," Amelia said, still giggling. "This is my big brother, Nathan. Nathan, this is the girl I was telling you about yesterday, Perdita."

"Perdy." I rolled my eyes as Tammie corrected Amelia with the shortened version everyone else used.

Nathan shook his head. "Perdita is much better." His eyes pierced into mine, and all of a sudden, I found it hard to breathe. My lips parted of their own accord. I couldn't even look away. I felt as though I was being hypnotised. I forgot the others were sitting there and just stared back at him, my stomach fluttering all over the place. My skin tingled with goose bumps, but he broke the spell by jumping to his feet and mumbling something under his breath. He hurried down to the back of the bus and sat there instead, leaving me wondering what just happened.

"Wow," Tammie said. "He's almost as bad as you, Perdy. Soul mate material or what." She burst out laughing at her own so *not* funny joke while Amelia looked at me as if I had done something to make her brother run off.

When we arrived at school, Dawn sidled up to Amelia.

"*So* sorry about yesterday," she said in her silkiest voice. "Just a little friendly teasing is all. No hard feelings, eh? I hope you sit with us at lunch today. We'd *love* to get to know you." She gave Amelia a winning smile, but nothing could penetrate the stony expression on Amelia's face.

"No thanks, I have plans," Amelia said, before linking arms with Tammie and me and walking into school with us, leaving Dawn standing there, open-mouthed with surprise. I saw Nathan shake his head at Amelia, looking amused. I didn't know if it was better or worse that he was the brother of my newest friend seeing as I had the beginnings of a major crush on him. Beginnings? Who was I kidding?

Whenever he looked in my direction it as though like he was generating massive heat waves and directing them straight at me. Apparently, I wasn't the only one he was having an effect on. The people who normally surrounded the likes of Dawn and Aaron had suddenly chosen him as their new leader or something. It was kind of creepy how they latched on to him. Maybe I was jealous that they got to spend time with him, but it was all very sheep like. I didn't have much of an identity, but at least I didn't share one with anyone else.

True to her word, Amelia sat with us at lunch. Joey was doing some sort of extra homework in an empty classroom, so he didn't show up, which gave Tammie and me the opportunity to get to know Amelia. Nathan stopped by our table and said hello but soon carried on across the room to sit with Dawn's crowd. They were more than happy to accept him into their fold. I hoped I hadn't been staring up at him as longingly as I had felt.

"No offense, Amelia, but your brother doesn't have the best taste in friends," Tammie said, looking mildly disgusted.

Amelia glanced over at her brother. "He's probably just trying to get to know as many people as possible."

"Where are you from, Amelia?" I asked, desperate to change the subject. I also desperately wanted to talk about Nathan, but I had to show some sort of self-control.

"Yeah, I can't tell by your accent," Tammie said, curious in spite of herself.

"We've moved around a lot. I've lived in Switzerland, South Africa, Canada, Austria, and Denmark. Plus we've stayed in France and Germany a lot to visit where my grandparents came from. We spent the last few years in England," Amelia said, rattling off countries as if they were nothing.

"Oh, you lucky thing," Tammie said.

Amelia shrugged. "It's nice seeing different places, but it would be better if we settled down, I think. It's hard to keep friends when you move on so much."

"Why did you move here?" Tammie asked. "It's not exactly buzzing with life."

"I'm not sure why we moved here in particular, but I like it, and the weather's pretty mild."

"Feels cold and wet to me." Tammie didn't bother hiding the scorn in her voice, and I worried in case Amelia would hate her.

"It could be a lot worse. Trust me," Amelia told her. "I hope we stay here this time." She sounded a little wistful, and I almost felt sorry for her. Travelling sounded like a great opportunity, but it must have been hard for her not having a permanent home. I was even more determined to make her feel welcome.

"Well, even if you move on, it'll be easy enough to stay in touch with us," I said, meaning it.

She grinned at me, and I was struck by something wholly familiar about her. I knew it would be easy to be friends with Amelia. After only a day, I felt as though I had known her for years. By the end of lunch, even Tammie was calling Amelia her new little sister. I was relieved to see Tammie liked her. Amelia was extremely nice, but Tammie could be contrary around other girls. I just hoped things would go as smoothly once Joey was around.

I saw Amelia a couple of times throughout the day. I was sort of keeping an eye on her, even if I wasn't exactly aware I was doing it. As far as I could tell, she wasn't getting hassle from anyone. It didn't hurt that her big brother was pretty popular already. I doubted anyone would bother her with anything other than trying to be her friend, although she didn't blend in as well as he did.

Nathan made a point of saying hello to Tammie and me if he passed us by in the hallway, much to the chagrin of Dawn. Even some of the others nodded at us in passing whenever he did it. It was sweet of him to make an effort to be nice to us when he was probably hearing all sorts of bad things about us from Dawn. It wouldn't have shocked me if he tried to stop his sister from spending time with us based on gossip, so I was pleasantly surprised by how he handled it.

Before the end of the day, he really surprised me. Scared me, in fact. I was busy rummaging frantically through my locker looking for my gold identity bracelet when he shoved it right in front of my face. I almost jumped out of my skin with fright. I had been so focused on my search that I hadn't even heard him next to me.

"Sorry," he said, trying not to laugh. "I found this in the hall earlier and remembered you had been wearing it on the bus. So, here you go."

"Oh." I took the bracelet from his extended hand, far too aware of the fact his fingers had touched mine. I jumped again at the tiny spark of energy I felt when his skin brushed against mine.

"Thanks. I was just looking for this."

He put his hand in his pocket. I looked at mine in wonder for a second.

"Glad to help," he said. It seemed as though he wanted to say something else, but one of his friends called him over. "See you later," he said before hurrying over to them.

I put my bracelet back on, wondering how on earth he had spotted it before. I was more than a little pleased he had noticed something about me. I was lucky he had found it. The catch was dodgy, and it occasionally fell off, but it usually ended up caught in my sleeve. That was the good thing about those heavy jumpers.

After school, I headed outside with Amelia and felt someone touch my wrist. Even before I turned my head, I knew it was Nathan, because I got that same rush of sensation under my skin.

"You should get that fixed," he said. I looked at my wrist and saw my bracelet was about to fall off again.

"Oh, yeah, thanks again," I said, my face heating up.

He gave me a wide smile that made my stomach feel as though it housed one hundred butterflies before he hurried ahead to join Aaron. I couldn't help smiling after him, but a prickly sensation on the back of my neck made me shudder—I felt as though someone was staring at me. Looking around, I saw a man with flame red hair leaning against a wall across the street. His head was turned in my direction, but I couldn't tell if it was really me he was looking at. I frowned and glanced at Amelia, meaning to ask her if she knew him, but when I looked back, he was gone.

My thoughts quickly wandered back to Nathan, even as I tried to concentrate on whatever Amelia was talking about. I couldn't stop mulling—and smiling—over that pleasant little jolt of energy I had felt before. Over-thinking everything Nathan Evans did was beginning to become a habit for me.

Dad was on late shifts for the rest of the week, so Gran and I ordered a takeaway that evening and watched a black and white film on the television. It was a pleasant distraction but didn't quite do the job completely. Thoughts of Nathan still managed to pop into my head unasked. As if she sensed my mind was on other things, Gran questioned me about my day numerous times.

"There are some new kids at school," I told her at last, hoping she would stop asking me if I gave her something.

"Were they mean to you?" she demanded.

"No, Gran," I said with a smile. "The boy is in my year. He seems nice. The girl is in the year below, but she sits with us at lunch and stuff. I like them."

"Ah," Gran said with a knowing smile. "So, is it the boy who's been on your mind all evening then?"

"Gran!" I tried not to laugh. "I've just been thinking about homework." I stuck my tongue out at her as she hmm-hmmed at me sceptically.

"You should ask them over some evening," she said.

"And inflict Dad on them? Yeah, right. Oh, meant to say, they moved into that big old house. You know, the one near the woods?"

"Really?" she said with interest. "I wonder what they've done with the place."

"Hmm. I doubt they'll stick around. Amelia told us today that they've lived all over the world but never anywhere for long. That's kind of sad, isn't it? Never having a real home?"

"Your home is where your family is, pet. They're probably all happy as long as they're together."

"Maybe. Doesn't work that way for all families though."

The corners of her mouth turned downward making me regret my words. I had obviously made her think of her daughter. My mother. The woman who didn't care where her family was. The woman whose home was as far away from her family as possible. I changed the subject quickly, although, I still thought Amelia longed for a real place to stay. A real place to call home.

That night I had one of *those* dreams, except this time, it turned into a nightmare. The figure was Nathan again, but that danger in the background that I always sensed came and took him away. He disappeared right in front of me.

I awoke upset and found it hard to get back to sleep. What bothered me most was how much the dreams affected me. I was completely obsessing over someone I didn't know. I had seen Tammie obsess over Joey. A lot. It wasn't pretty. But at least she knew him. This was a stranger I was dreaming about. That had to be weird.

It took a while to realise *why* I was feeling so upset. It wasn't because I was dreaming about Nathan. I liked dreaming about him. I liked thinking about him. I liked liking him. I was upset because something bad had happened to him in the stupid dream. It was as though I couldn't shake the idea that something about the dream was real. Sleep evaded me that night because I couldn't help worrying something bad might actually happen to him.

Chapter Four

The next morning, it didn't take Tammie long to realise I was not in a great humour. She didn't bother asking why, probably assuming my Gran and Dad had been fighting again. On the bus, I was quieter than usual. I still hadn't shaken the awful feeling my dream had given me. Amelia and Nathan sat with us. He was right across from me again. I barely said hello to them, but I couldn't help looking up at him to see what made him so different, why he had such a big impact on me.

The dream had really spooked me, and I couldn't let it go. Between my dreams and how I felt when he barely touched me, I struggled to find a reasonable explanation for it all. He noticed me staring and looked right back at me, bemused.

"Perdita, are you okay?" Amelia asked, concern obvious in her voice. I gave her a quick nod.

"Ah, don't mind her. She's a bit grumpy this morning," Tammie joked.

I slumped back in my chair, avoiding all of their eyes as I put my earphones on and turned up the sound. I tried to tune out the bewildered glances they all exchanged. It wasn't long before Nathan left to sit with the others down the back. I stretched out my legs and waited for the journey to be over. The music was loud enough to block out my thoughts but not the cold shivery feeling I'd had all morning.

I kept the earphones on even as I walked into my first class. Nathan tried to get my attention, but I kept my eyes directed at the floor as I passed him by. I sat down, but he followed me and took out my earphones. Switching off the music, I stared back at him in confusion as he knelt beside me.

"Are you sure you're okay?" he said in a low voice, one arm leaning on the back of my chair. I nodded, unsure of what to say. He was a little too close to me. Not that I was complaining.

"You can tell me if anything is bothering you, you know." He moved his hand so it rested lightly on my shoulder. He looked right at me, expecting a reply. I could hardly tell him what was bothering me, but I wanted to share something with him because he seemed so concerned. If I was really rude, he might never bother again.

I rubbed my eyes. "I'm just tired is all. I had a screwed up dream last night and I…" I hesitated when I saw Dawn and her groupies walk into the room. "I'm fine," I said firmly.

"Well, cheer up then. You don't look as pretty when you're miserable."

My smile was automatic and genuine. He grinned back at me and handed me my earphones before taking his usual seat. The cold, sickening feeling in my stomach transformed into something warm and comforting. I was still smiling when Tammie sat next to me.

"Bit of a hormone imbalance today, yeah?" she said.

I pushed against her and looked down at my book, still smirking to myself. Cheered up beyond belief, the icky feelings were all but forgotten. Amelia seemed surprised when I grinned at her in the hallway, but she didn't comment. She didn't even remark when she caught Nathan winking at me in the hallway.

Joey finally met Amelia for the first time at lunch when she joined us at our table.

"Joey, this is Amelia. Her brother's the new kid in our year. Amelia, this is my cousin Joey. He thinks he's the boss of me, but obviously, I rule."

Joey barely heard me, he was too busy checking out Amelia. His eyes lit up when he shook her hand. Tammie's face clouded over. Major warning sign right there. I made sure Amelia sat on the other side of me so Joey was sandwiched between me and Tammie. She sat as close to him as possible and pretty much demanded all of his attention, so I figured we had avoided a hissy fit.

"By the way, the stud we found for Dolly is coming to stay with us this week," Joey told me after a few minutes.

"Does that mean I get a pup?" I had once been promised one, but my Dad was always changing his mind.

"First choice," Joey said. I was thrilled—a pup might be better company than Dad and Gran.

"What kind of dog?" Amelia asked.

"She's a boxer. Tan with white socks and nose." Joey sounded like a proud parent. "Male is brindle, so you should have some choices, Perdy."

"Oh, cool," Amelia said.

"Would you be interested in a pup? I'm sure I could work something out for you." Joey's tone was far too flirty. I groaned at his lack of awareness, imagining I could feel poison seep from Tammie's pores.

Amelia shook her head. "We already have a few dogs."

"Ah, I see," he said, holding her wrist still for a second to peer at the silver charm bracelet that dangled there. "Is that why you've so many dog charms then?"

She smirked. "They're not dogs. They're werewolves."

Tammie's eyebrows rose. "Werewolves?"

Knowing her as well as I did, I guessed it was time to change the subject or else a smart alec comment would be next.

"So, what kind of dogs do you have, Amelia?" I said.

"Wolfhounds."

"They must be bigger than you." Spite dripped from her Tammie's words.

"Almost. You all should come to my house and see them." Amelia seemed oblivious to the danger.

That had Tammie interested. She was dying to see what the house looked like on the inside, but Joey ruined it by acting altogether too interested himself. There was a fine line in Tammie's eyes, and he had crossed it. She drummed her long fingernails on the table loudly, a deep scowl marring her features.

"I doubt your parents would want half the town nosing around your house already," I said, desperate to distract Tammie.

Amelia's smile fell. "Actually, my parents are dead. I live with my grandparents and uncle instead."

"You have something in common with Perdy then. She has a granny instead of a mammy too." The malice in Tammie's voice was unmistakeable this time.

"Tammie!" Joey looked as shocked as I felt. "What the hell?"

Tammie could be mean sometimes, but that was too far. Amelia's eyes glittered, so I stood and asked her to walk to the shop with me to give her an excuse to leave. She nodded and hurried toward the canteen doors.

"Jesus, Tammie. Could you be any more of a bitch?" I hissed under my breath before following Amelia, all too aware of Nathan's head turning in our direction.

"You okay?" I asked as we walked down the hall. She nodded, but I saw a tear fall. I put an arm around her, hoping to comfort her.

"Aw, please don't get upset. I'm sorry about Tammie. She's just jealous and gets a bit thick sometimes. She doesn't think about what she says."

"I'm fine," she insisted, wiping a tear from her cheek. "I don't even know why I'm upset."

"Well, it's understandable to be sad about it."

"It happened years ago, it's not even... I'm not... I don't know why that got to me," she said, shaking her head.

"A lot is going on for you. New home, new school, new people. Some not so nice people. Only natural to feel a little bit more emotional than usual." I felt so bad for her. She was obviously a sensitive person, and now she kept having to deal with people who didn't care if they upset her. "It'll be okay. Things will get easier, and you'll settle in and feel like you were always here."

She nodded, drying her eyes. "You're right. I'm just feeling a bit overwhelmed or something today."

I caught a better look at her bracelet. It was covered in tiny charms that looked like wolves.

"Don't you like any animals other than wolves?" I said with a smile, hoping to cheer her up.

"Werewolves," she corrected. Her eyes locked onto mine, not a hint of a smile on her face. I couldn't help shivering—not that I believed her. We were interrupted before I could figure out what to say.

"Amelia?" Nathan caught up with us.

She blinked away the last of her tears. "It's okay, Nathan. I'm fine."

"What happened?" He frowned at me when he asked, as if he thought I had done something to upset her.

"Nothing important. Perdita took care of me. I'm fine now, I promise." She sounded reassuring, but he still didn't relax.

"Are you sure?"

She nodded again. Nathan's concern was a little odd, or maybe I just wasn't used to siblings looking out for each other.

"Well… okay then." He seemed reluctant to leave. "Thanks for… being there for her."

I nodded. I didn't trust myself to say actual words that made sense in front of him.

Amelia sniffled loudly. "I have to go to the bathroom for a sec. Wait for me, please?" she asked me.

"Yeah, sure," I said. She ran off and left us standing together. He didn't look happy.

"So, what really happened then?" he said, his eyes narrowing coldly.

Why did he have to ask me questions that required vocal answers?

"Um, my friend made a stupid remark about me and Amelia having something in common because we don't have mothers, and Amelia got upset." For some reason I was afraid to say it.

"Yours is dead too?"

"Oh, no, sorry!" I was embarrassed to have made it sound like my story even came close to comparing with theirs. "Mine just didn't want me." I closed my eyes for a second, wincing a bit at how pathetic that sounded out loud.

"I'm sorry."

"Oh. It's not a big deal," I said hurriedly. "I mean, not like you… sorry, what I meant was it isn't upsetting for me. She was never around, so I don't miss her or anything. That's obviously nowhere near as bad as what's happened to you and Amelia. I'm really sorry about your parents."

"It wasn't recent," he said, his voice soft as he moved closer. "But Amelia, she's…."

"Sensitive?" I offered.

"Yeah, exactly. I have to look out for her a lot. Our mother was murdered, so…." He stopped talking and looked at me blankly as if he didn't know quite what to say. It was as though he had the world on his shoulders, so I touched his arm lightly without thinking.

"It's okay. I'll look out for her when you're not there," I reassured him. I wasn't sure why I said it or even why I felt compelled to look out for Amelia. There was something about them both that made me feel as though I knew them well. Hearing their mother had been murdered just strengthened the connection I felt.

He smiled at me gratefully. I was starting to feel sort of normal around him. He moved even closer to me, and I realised my hand was still on his arm. My fingers stung with the heat. It was just like before, except this was a slow, lingering burn rather than a quick shock. I held on for too long, but I couldn't move away. I didn't want to.

"Thank you, Perdita. It means a lot that you're a friend to her." He spoke so quietly I could barely hear him. Not that I was paying much attention to what he was saying, I was too busy staring at him all dreamy-eyed. Something about the way he said my name put me in a little bit of a trance.

"Oh, look. How *cute*. Our resident freak thinks she actually has a chance with Nate."

I whipped my hand away and stepped back quickly, not needing to look around. I already knew Dawn was sneering at me. She pulled Abbi in front of me, knocking me backward in the process. She made sure I saw the flirty grin she directed at Nathan. My fingers itched with a compulsion to pull her to the ground by her hair.

Dawn casually rested her hand on Nathan's chest. "Ready to walk us to our next class?"

The bell rang and Nathan checked his watch with a frown. "I suppose I better go…." He looked over at me, so I nodded at him to let him know I would wait for Amelia. I got the feeling he didn't want anyone else to know she was upset.

"Thanks again, Perdita," he said before he walked off, followed by Dawn and Abbi. Abbi looked behind her and gave me a quick sympathetic smile, but my good humour disappeared.

Amelia wasn't long. Her eyes were a little less red looking. "Where did Nathan go?"

"Ah, Dawn came and claimed him." I tried to look cheerful.

She rolled her eyes. "I should disown him for being mates with her."

"She can be nice when she feels like it. I mean, she's popular for a reason," I told Amelia as we walked toward our classrooms.

"Yeah, 'cos she's a scary biatch. I meant what I said earlier by the way, about you all coming over. You anyway. You could come over for dinner or something."

"Shouldn't you let your family know before you start inviting random strangers to your house?" I reminded her.

"You *so* don't count as a stranger." She said it lightly, but again, the intensely serious look on her face unsettled me. She gave a little wave and hurried off to her side of the building leaving me wondering.

Too agitated to think straight, I strolled to my own class. The only thoughts in my head were how it felt to be so close to Nathan, and yet how easy it was for people like Dawn to stand in front of me. The story of my life, and it was about time I changed it. Tammie hadn't exactly helped my mood by being so unnecessarily nasty to Amelia.

As soon as I stepped into my classroom, Dawn burst into exaggerated giggles. Her laughter felt like razor blades running across my skin. She was so obvious about everything. I felt like sneering right back at her, instead I eyed her as boldly as I dared. She whispered loudly to some of the people next to her, invoking the predictable chorus of laughter. Aaron Hannigan observed me with some interest as if I had just been born that second in front of him.

"Settle down," the teacher said. "As for you, Ms. Rivers, you're late."

I shrugged. "Sorry."

As I walked past some of the desks to get to an empty seat, Dawn pushed her school bag into my path. I kicked it back under her desk with an enormous amount of satisfaction.

"Eh, do you mind?" she said, loud enough for everyone to hear.

"Eh, do you mind keeping your shit to yourself?" I didn't stutter, and it felt great.

Dawn whirled around to look at her friends. "The cheek of that one."

Nathan and Aaron both looked mildly amused, but the girls all gasped in mock horror.

Tammie grinned up at me, but I walked straight past her and sat at an empty table. I needed to be alone. I didn't know exactly what was wrong with me, but I figured it was a little of everything. Tammie's treatment of Amelia because she was jealous, Nathan making me think it might be possible he liked me a little and then running off with anyone who demanded his attention, and finally Dawn's incessant needling. It hadn't been just that week; she had always tried her best to make either myself or Tammie feel stupid or insecure.

Tammie tried in vain to catch my eye throughout the rest of the class, but I was busy working myself up into a tight ball of rage. As soon as the bell rang, she was up and in front of my desk, blocking my way so I would have to speak to her.

"Are you seriously going to start ignoring me now?"

I wasn't in the habit of standing up to my Dad or Dawn, but I had never done it to Tammie either. I was sick of being a doormat for everyone. I had to admit I might have been a *tiny* bit hormonal, or hormental as Tammie liked to say.

"Just leave me alone. I'm not in the humour for this." I tried to warn her, but she had to push it. Just because she could. That usually worked with me, but things were changing. *I* was changing.

"You're going to pick a new kid over me? Some friend you are!"

"Piss off Tamara. You're the one always forcing people to pick sides, and now that I think about it, you're the only one *making* sides. Would you ever stop and cop on and think about what you say for a change? Why do you have to be a bitch for absolutely no reason? And how could you bring up my Mam like that? You know I hate talking about her. And comparing that whole thing with someone whose mother died just to make them feel bad was low, even for you!"

The ever shrinking sensible part of me deep inside was screaming at me to shut up, or at least calm down, but I was on a roll.

"Perdy, settle down," Joey said, getting involved as always and riling me up even more.

"Is this your business? Just because you don't have the balls to stick up for anyone else doesn't mean it has to run in the family, you know."

Visibly taken aback, he was probably a little hurt, but I was beyond caring. Dawn pretty much cackled behind him. "So funny when the loners turn on each other."

I pointed my finger at her, furious now. "If you don't shut the fu…"

"Okay, relax girls," Nathan interrupted, standing in front of me with his arms out like he was shielding Dawn.

"What are you, her bodyguard?"

He laughed at me. He actually laughed at me. I was seconds away from exploding, and he had to go and laugh at me. What kind of an idiot laughs at someone on a rampage? Dawn peeked out from behind him with the most annoyingly smug expression I had ever seen. My hand itched to slap it off her face.

"Don't mind him," Tammie said. "He's just as bad as her. Let's go."

She pulled me by the arm, taking advantage of the situation the second my anger was directed elsewhere. I followed without thinking, glaring at Nathan as I stormed past him. His forehead wrinkled, but he moved out of our way.

"Girls," Joey muttered, picking up our bags and shuffling after us. Out in the hall, Tammie made a show of giving me a big hug when the others walked by. I was still vibrating with anger. She held me tight while Dawn looked me up and down, as if sensing I was at snapping point and might do something that would get me into a lot of trouble with my Dad.

"Let's go shopping or something," she whispered in my ear.

"What, now?"

"Yeah, why not? We could use a break. Joey will cover for us."

Joey sighed when she asked for his help but agreed to try and keep us out of trouble. I was more than willing to get out of school because I was close to tears. The anger I had been feeling had floated away, leaving me with an awful feeling of melancholy and a lump in my throat. All I could think about was how Nathan had pretty much protected Dawn from me. She was the bully and tormentor in our year, and he was protecting her from me? It was one of those days—I knew if I didn't get away from everyone that I'd go completely overboard and say or do something I would absolutely regret.

I sent Amelia a text letting her know we were ditching. I hoped she wouldn't be mad at me for kind of rowing with her brother and being friends with Tammie again already. She didn't text me back, so I figured she was probably annoyed at me.

We snuck out of school and caught a bus into town. It's a lot easier to ditch when you don't have a school uniform. It was the first time I had ever left school when I wasn't supposed to, but I was tired of worrying about rules. It was nice to make a choice for myself for a change.

Our first stop was a chocolate milkshake in a fast food restaurant on Grafton Street. We sat there for at least an hour, sharing chips and getting funny looks from the cleaning staff.

"So, what's the deal with you, Perdy?" Tammie said at last. "You're acting so different lately. Even before today, I mean. I get today, well, sort of. But what's going on with you?"

I shrugged. "Dunno. Just feel different."

"You flipped out a bit earlier," she said, hesitant, as if she was afraid I'd lose it on her.

I couldn't help laughing. "Yeah, I did a bit. I blame Dawn. Everywhere I turn, she's there mocking me over something. It's starting to get in on me."

"I thought you were going to smack her one," Tammie said, her face lighting up at the memory.

"I don't know what I was going to do."

"Then stupid new boy stepped in and ruined it." Tammie made a face; she had always wanted to see somebody smack Dawn Talbot hard.

I made a face too but for different reasons.

"I think she's jealous of you," Tammie said.

I spluttered into my milkshake. "You what?"

"Really. I think she's getting at you because she likes Nathan."

"What's that got to do with me?"

"Well, you're making friends with his sister, so you'll probably be around him. And he looks at you an awful lot."

I rolled my eyes. "No, he doesn't. And lots of people are going to be friends with his sister. Doesn't mean a thing."

"I'm just saying. I think she's afraid he's going to like you instead of her. I would be, if I was her."

I looked at Tammie like she had four heads. "Are we living in two different worlds or what? He sits with her, not me. He talks to her, not me. He picked up for her, not me. Think it's pretty clear she has no worries. Besides, she was getting at me long before Nathan Evans came along."

"That's 'cos you were friends with me. This is different. As for him, maybe he's shy. Just because he sits with all them doesn't mean he likes her. And I think he was just stepping in to calm everyone down. I don't think he was really picking up for anyone, Perdy." She looked thoughtful for a minute. "You know, it would *really* annoy Dawn if he liked you."

"No!"

She flinched. "What? I haven't even suggested anything yet!" She tried to look innocent, but the fit of husky laughter she burst into ruined the effect. I knew Tammie too well; she would have enjoyed it if I tried to make Nathan like me just to ruin Dawn's day.

"Don't even think about it, okay? Besides, I reckon there's more chance of him liking Abbi than Dawn."

"How do you figure that?" she said, frowning.

"Abbi is prettier than Dawn, and she's nicer too."

Tammie looked horrified.

"I don't mean she's nice," I amended. "Just that she's not as evil as Dawn."

Tammie considered this. "She *is* prettier. Dawn's lips are too thin, and her eyes are a bit sly and squinty. But he doesn't seem to notice any of them in that kind of way. Maybe he has a thing for redheads," she added with a grin. "I wonder would Amelia know. I'm going to ask her."

"No, you're not. And while we're on the subject, you have to be nicer to Amelia," I lectured.

She was wise enough to look abashed. "Okay, so I *was* trying to be mean to her before, but you *saw* Joey. He's going to like her. I just know it."

"So what? That doesn't mean anything. Anyway, if you like him so much then tell him instead of chasing off anyone who hasn't even expressed an interest yet."

"I can't." She shook her head.

"Why? What's the worst that could happen? At least you'll know and stop living in limbo land."

"Worst that could happen... let me think. Oh, yeah, he doesn't like me back, it gets all awkward, and then we can't even be friends?" She was a little too sarcastic for my liking.

"Just tell him. Or jump on him. I don't know. But get it over and done with before somebody else does, and you miss your chance. How can you win if you're acting like you're not in the race?"

She stared at me, considering. "Do you really think someone else will get stuck in if I don't?"

I hesitated. "Well, some day, yeah. I don't think girls are going to be kicking down his door or anything, but imagine if one of Dawn's crowd took a liking to him. And they ended up getting married or something. Then we'd be stuck with them forever all because you couldn't tell him you liked him." I sat back and watched her face tense up. I knew mentioning the D word would get her going.

"Oh, my God. I am not going to be his bridesmaid. I'd have to be his bridesmaid, Perdy. And *then*, then they'd throw the bouquet thing, and I wouldn't catch it, and I'd live alone forever except for all my cats. I'd be a cat lady." Tammie frowned. "No, wait, I hate cats. I'd be Miss Havisham!"

"Who?"

"You know, the one who sits in her wedding dress forever. I'd buy a dress and wear it all the time, except my house wouldn't be mouldy."

She went bizarrely far with my scenario, but whatever worked was fine with me. She was way too possessive over Joey without actually staking a claim, and I knew the only way for her to accept Amelia into our group was if Tammie became too busy trying to catch Joey's eye.

She stopped hyperventilating long enough to grin at me wickedly. "So, I guess that means you can't get mad at Dawn, considering you haven't told Nathan you're interested in him."

My frown was so deep I could barely see her. "I never said I was interested in anybody."

"Oh, please! Don't even think about denying it. You can't even say a full sentence when he's around. You nearly wet yourself if he smiles at you. You. Are. Smitten."

"I'll have you know I've already said a few sentences to him." It was pretty much true.

She patted my arm. "Sure you did. You lurve him."

"I don't. I just… he's quite easy on the eye is all."

She snorted with laughter. "Easy on the eye? Sure, that's all it is. Don't get in denial about it; I've known you for years, and I've never seen you like this before. You can barely look at him without blushing."

"Oh, so what! He'll say something stupid tomorrow, and I won't like him anymore. Big deal." I slumped back in my chair feeling annoyed. I hoped he wouldn't say anything stupid.

Tammie's eyes grew wide. "You really *do* like him, don't you?"

I shrugged. I didn't want to fuel those particular flames, but I couldn't exactly lie about it either. At least not in a believable way.

"Aw, poor you. It's going to be hard hanging around with his sister when you like him," she said.

"No bother. I'll be over it in a few days."

"What, like me?" she said softly.

I gulped. I saw her point. She had started off with a tiny crush that progressed into a full on obsession with my cousin. And he wasn't even good looking. I must have looked stricken because she leaned over and gave me a hug.

"It'll be okay, Perdy. He's noticed you. It'll be different for you," she said, but her reassurance didn't work on me.

"Like I said before, we must be living in two different worlds. Now, when are you going to talk to Joey?"

She paled at the thought. "I need something new to wear. And somewhere to go. And someone else to tell him for me." We giggled together until one of the cleaners cleared their throat and wiped down our table for the fifth or sixth time. We decided it was time to start shopping.

We wandered up Grafton Street, stopping to listen to the occasional busker. At the entrance to Stephen's Green Shopping Centre, a man gave me a leery smile. I might not have noticed him, but his eyes were a strangely yellow shade of amber that attracted my attention. He seemed familiar, but it wasn't until we passed him by that I remembered he had been standing across from our school the day before. I looked back to check, but I couldn't see him anymore and assumed I had been mistaken.

We spent the rest of the day trawling the clothes shops and picking up a couple of sale bargains. For once, shopping cheered me up a little. Until I got home.

Gran was waiting for me in the kitchen. "What did you get?" she said, spying my bag. I shoved it at her. She looked at the contents and nodded.

"So, is this where you were during your last couple of classes today?" she asked sternly.

I groaned and sank into a chair across from her.

"Indeed. Your school rang me and asked where you were. I told them you had come home sick with my permission. Do you have a good reason for me to lie for you, or should I call them straight back with the truth?"

"Ah, Gran, stop. I didn't ask you to lie. I was having a really bad day, okay? I was ready to hit someone, so I figured it would be better to step away than end up in trouble for flipping out at school."

She studied me for a couple of minutes. "That actually sounds like a good reason to me. The real problem is your father. What's stopping me from telling him the truth? Nothing. At least, not yet."

Her eyes took on a mischievous glint, and I knew she was up for making a deal.

"What do you want?" I asked, wary because I knew she would think of something either ridiculous or embarrassing. Probably both.

"I want you to wear your hair down for the rest of the week," she said with a cheeky grin. "And no navy jumpers either. In fact, no dark clothes at all. I want you to look like a girl for the whole week."

"Gran!" I protested. "You're not serious!"

"I'm deadly serious. Unless you want your father to have you homeschooled for going on the hop?"

I couldn't believe my grandmother sometimes. But knowing her, this was my only choice. I hated wearing my hair down, but at least I would be able to sort of hide behind it. The clothes part wouldn't be too bad, but she reaped some kind of sadistic pleasure from me bringing attention on myself. When she was younger, she worked as a club singer and had long, dark red hair like mine. She always brushed my hair and said it was wasted on me because I didn't use it to my advantage. Whatever that meant.

I ran upstairs to hide my shopping bag from my Dad and decided to give Amelia a call. I was still afraid she was mad at me.

"Hey, Amelia. It's Perdy."

"Oh, hey."

"Um… you didn't text me back earlier."

"Yeah, sorry, I didn't have credit. Did you get anything nice?" She sounded chirpy enough.

"You're not angry at me?"

"Why would I be angry?" She laughed down the phone. It was a complete relief.

"Oh. Well, 'cos I kind of got pissy with your brother when he picked up for Dawn before, and then I went off with Tammie even though I wasn't really talking to her. My head was just melted. I needed to get out of there before I threw something at Dawn."

"Hold on. He picked up for Dawn? What, like, against you?"

"Yeah, well, sort of. It was no big deal, but I *did* snap at him, and I figured he told you, and you weren't impressed with me. I don't want to fall out…"

"No, of course not! And Tammie's your friend, so I'd hardly expect you to avoid her over one comment. Like you said, she just didn't think."

"But I *was* avoiding her, until we had a row, and then the whole class seemed to get involved. Anyway, not the point. The thing is, there was a reason she was mean to you. I'm not saying that's an excuse, but she wanted to hurt you because she thought Joey liked you. She's always liked him, but she's too afraid to make the first move. We had a bit of a chat about it, it won't happen again." I hoped.

"Oh." Amelia was silent for a moment. "Oh, well, that makes a lot of sense. Maybe we can nudge him in the right direction then!"

We chatted for a little while longer about how we could get Tammie and Joey together before we finally hung up. I was delighted she was still talking to me, and even better, she wasn't holding a grudge against Tammie. I was glad to have her as a friend. The fact her brother was hot didn't exactly hurt either.

Chapter Five

ammie and I were both feeling nervous about sitting in front of Amelia and Nathan the next morning for similar reasons. They sat opposite us, an awkward atmosphere immediately filling the air. I tried to look as apologetic as I could, but I was too freaked about having my hair down to concentrate on doing a good job. Gran had insisted upon me holding up my end of our stupid deal. Tammie opened her mouth to start saying sorry to Amelia, but I had to interrupt.

"I'm sorry, just everyone hold that thought for a sec. Amelia, do you have a loan of a hair band or clip, or something I can put my hair up with? Please say you do. Tammie's refusing to help me."

"Don't give her anything!" Tammie shouted. "Sorry." She lowered her voice. "But just don't do it!"

"What on earth is going on?" Amelia said.

"My Gran found out about us ditching yesterday, and in exchange for not ratting me out to my Dad, she's made a deal with me. Her silence, if I wear my hair down for the rest of the week. I know. She's insane. She even checked my bag and pockets this morning and confiscated everything I was sneaking into school." I was nearly in tears by the end.

Amelia glanced at Nathan and burst into laughter. "I can't wait to meet your Gran. How cool is she?"

"No, Amelia. *Insane.* Insane is the word to describe her. So can you help me out?"

She shook her head. "Even if I wanted to, which I don't by the way, I don't have anything with me. Sorry!"

"Are you done? Can I say my bit now? Is that okay with you?" Tammie asked me snottily. I nodded, feeling a little bit desperate with the need to plait my hair back.

Tammie launched into a long spiel of an apology that Amelia took gracefully. They did all the girly squealing that went along with making friends again. They were so intent on their conversation that it felt like Nathan and I were alone together.

He leaned forward just as I opened my mouth to try and apologise to him. "Oh, wait," I said. "I just need to say something really quick before you go."

He sat there quietly while I spoke. "I have to say sorry about yesterday. I was in bad form all round and snapped at everyone within viewing distance. I was a total bitch and took it out on you too, so, sorry." I took a deep breath and winced, not sure if he'd tell me to get lost or not.

He shook his head, putting his hand on my knee in a completely absent-minded way. "No, I was about to say sorry to you," he insisted. I tried to ignore his hand and leaned forward to focus on his words.

"My sister told me you thought I was taking Dawn's side or something, but I wasn't, I swear. I was just trying to calm everyone down. Obviously laughing in the middle of it wasn't the best move, but you looked so cute when you were all outraged at me that I couldn't help it."

I grinned at him, and he tugged on my loose hair a little. "Obviously I think you're cuter when you're not thinking about physically harming me." I tried not to laugh at that but failed miserably.

He leaned a little closer and lowered his voice to a whisper. "By the way, you shouldn't worry about your hair. It suits you like that." I imagined myself melting into my seat because that's literally how I felt. He glanced at my mouth, and I caught my breath, convinced he was about to kiss me right there on the bus.

"Oh, get a room already!" Tammie said with a snort, abruptly ruining the moment. We both pulled backward automatically. He looked at his hand on my knee with the kind of horror that could have been explained had his hand been unexpectedly amputated. He didn't even bother with a mumbled excuse; he just hurried down to the back of the bus.

Tammie raised her eyebrows at me, but all I could do was glare back at her. Amelia, on the other hand, was grinning broadly. I hid behind my hair and concentrated on ignoring them both. Although I was glad they were getting on, I wasn't exactly having a great morning. First the hair thing. Super annoying when your hair is long and thick and completely inconvenient. Then Nathan. I mean, did he really have to look so traumatised when he noticed his hand was on my knee?

I spent most of the day having my hair pulled. It wasn't as sweet when Nathan wasn't the one doing it. In fact, it was extremely irritating. Dawn always wore her hair down, and I had never seen anyone pull her hair over it. They were just picking on me because I wasn't as scary. Or maybe they wanted to see me lose the rag again. Either way, I didn't win. Dawn made many, many scathing remarks throughout the day. I made a mental note to throw something at her the very next time she said the word ginger.

At lunch time, Joey took one look at me before remarking, "What the hell happened to your hair?"

"Charming."

"How do *I* look?" Tammie said, out of the blue. I had to bite the inside of my cheek to stop myself from laughing at the surprised expression on Joey's face. He peered at Tammie as if it was the first time he had ever seen her.

"You always look nice," he replied, quite sensibly. He was nowhere near as charming as Nathan, but he managed to put a smile on Tammie's face.

"Get a room," Amelia whispered cheekily, but Joey didn't hear her. Tammie blushed but still seemed pretty pleased with herself.

Nathan sat next to Amelia for a few minutes before lunch ended. She introduced Joey as my cousin.

"Cousin?" Nathan said, looking at me for confirmation, so I nodded.

"See? I told you." Amelia sounded triumphant.

I must have looked as confused as I felt because Amelia decided to carry on with an explanation.

"Oh, Nathan thought Joey was your boyfriend," she said, beaming at me. Nathan made a choking sound. "But I thought he was Tammie's," she added quickly. This time, Tammie looked physically sick.

"Really?" Joey said. He didn't seem unhappy with that notion. In fact, it was as though the idea had occurred to him for the very first time if the way he looked at Tammie was anything to go by. Nathan, on the other hand, was already on his feet and edging away from us, his face a little pink.

"What on earth is his deal?" I said, when he sat down at his usual table.

"Ask him," Amelia piped up.

I was about to answer her when somebody pulled my hair yet again. I spun around in my seat to see Aaron Hannigan grin at me as he passed by our table.

"Is there a full moon or something? The school's gone mad this week."

"Aw, it's not so bad," Tammie said. "At least things are halfway to interesting. You're always complaining how boring everything is. Quit moaning, and enjoy."

"Easy for you to say," I said under my breath. I couldn't figure Nathan out, and it bothered me more than I liked to admit. One minute he was overly familiar with me, the next he was running off. All the damn time. His mood swings were making me dizzy. He was so unpredictable that I was permanently on edge, waiting for something to happen already.

After school, he trailed behind us as we strolled to the car park, but he didn't speak to me until the following morning after we had all gotten off the bus. He pulled me aside and told the others to go on ahead, then, when nobody was looking, handed me a brand new packet of hair things. I stared up at him, but he kept messing at his own hair and avoiding my eyes.

"I noticed you seemed a little tormented by the hair thing yesterday, so I figured it would be the same today. I thought I'd sneak you some contraband," he said, shrugging his shoulders. To my horror, real tears formed in my eyes. I started to hug him then realised what I was doing and backed away hastily.

"Sorry," I mumbled. "I mean, thanks. For this. That's really… thoughtful."

"Maybe people will leave you alone today. Come on, we're going to be late for class."

I ripped the packet open as we walked and pulled my hair back into a loose ponytail while he carried my bag. We stepped into the hallway, but I noticed his group of friends in the corridor ahead so pre-empted his usual escape. I took my bag and pushed him ahead.

"Go on," I said with a grin. "And thanks. Seriously."

He smiled back at me before stopping, his forehead creasing into a frown. "Could you do me a favour and not tell anyone about this? I have a hardcore reputation to maintain here, ya know?" I almost believed him until I saw the laughter in his eyes.

I couldn't help smirking. "I'll keep your secret, macho man."

"Cheers."

I knew I had a big dopey grin on my face as he walked away, but I couldn't help it.

Tammie tutted in annoyance when I sat down next to her in class. "Where did you get that from?" she said, pointing at my hair.

"Turns out I have better friends than you," I said, unable to resist the urge to stick my tongue out at her.

That afternoon, Amelia asked me to keep her company after school while Nathan had a trial football training session with the boys in our year. It wasn't a school team, but they were allowed to use the grounds for training because one of the teachers was their trainer. We wandered up and down the length of the pitch, pretending to be interested while the boys showed off in front of Nathan. According to Amelia, they were desperate for him to join the team.

As soon as he started playing, I could see why. He was surprisingly fast and agile—all good things. He seemed a lot more skilful than the others too, running rings around Aaron Hannigan who was well known as the team's best player. I wasn't usually interested in football, but it was kind of cool to watch him effortlessly own the ball.

"Wow, he's pretty good," I said.

Amelia nodded. "Yup. Back where we used to live, before he was expelled, he was captain of the school team."

I stared at her, but she didn't elaborate. I wondered what he had done to get expelled. Maybe schools in England were really strict.

By the end of the match, Aaron's face was red with a temper. He was the only one who didn't praise Nathan.

Nathan ran over to us before he got changed. "Sorry that took so long," he said, panting, his face flushed from the exercise.

"Looks like Aaron has some competition." I gestured toward Aaron.

Nathan looked around and saw how unhappy Aaron was for the first time. "He'll get over it. It's a team game, we all count."

"So you're definitely joining them then?" I asked.

He nodded, taking a long drink from a bottle of water his sister handed him. My mobile rang just as he opened his mouth to speak again. It was my Dad. I had a sinking feeling in my stomach; I had forgotten he wasn't in work and hadn't told him I'd be home late.

"Perdy, where the hell are you?" I could almost see his frown through the phone.

"Sorry, Dad. I forgot to ring. I'm still at school. Amelia's brother was training, so she didn't want to be left alone out here."

"You're supposed to come straight home after school. I've been worried sick about you!"

"I said sorry. I forgot you were home."

"That's no excuse. You should be home whether I'm here or not."

"All right, Dad. I'm on my way." I hung up with a frustrated tut. "Sorry, Amelia. I have to go."

"Did you get in trouble?" Amelia asked.

"Sort of. My Dad's strict about stuff. I better go. I'll see you tomorrow. Good luck with the football, Nathan."

I hurried away, barely waving goodbye, I was so embarrassed. My Dad had kicked up such a fuss about me being an hour late. I wasn't that far from my 17th birthday. It was mortifying.

I was so flustered that I walked straight into a man outside the school. "Sorry," I mumbled, hurrying to the bus stop. It wasn't until I was on the bus that I realised it was the same red haired man I had seen a couple of times. I had a vague sense of there being something odd about him, but I was too worried about what my Dad was going to say to think about a complete stranger too deeply.

At home, I suffered through a particularly long lecture. Apologising didn't shorten it at all. Dad was on a roll.

"If I can't trust you, then how am I supposed to give you more freedom, Perdy? Well?"

"Dad. I'm sorry. But I was at school. What on earth do you think is going to happen there? There are a lot of bad things I could be doing, but I'm not. Give me a bit of credit, please."

"Bad things can happen anywhere," he said sternly. "I want you to be responsible. Is that so bad? I don't want to see you make the same mistakes as…"

I held up my hands. "Okay, stop. I'm not like her, so don't talk to me about her, all right?"

I turned my back on him and ran up to my room, my hands shaking. I was being punished for the mistakes my mother had made. That wasn't fair. Me staying late at school was nowhere near as bad as her running out on her family. He knew I hated talking about her, so bringing her up in the middle of a lecture was low.

Chapter Six

Weeks seemed to fly by. I was still a bit cool with my Dad, but he dealt with it well and even stopped ringing me every five minutes whenever I wasn't in his line of sight. He was trying to make things up with me after our row, but a simple sorry would have been enough. He would never admit when he was in the wrong.

Nathan flitted between our company and the cooler group although he didn't spend as much time with us as them. His popularity grew, especially after the football team won their first match all year. He had scored, but I wasn't allowed go. Another reason I wasn't on the best of terms with my Dad.

Amelia and Joey kept a safe distance from each other on either side of Tammie. It helped when some kids in Amelia's year began to sit with us occasionally. Tammie seemed to feel as though the threat was gone. She launched into a full blown flirtation attempt with Joey. She sometimes seemed frustrated that he hadn't asked her out yet, but he was definitely thinking of her as a girl. I could see things slowly changing between them.

It was amazing, but at school, time was exaggerated. Relationships could begin and end in a day. So it wasn't really surprising that in a mere three weeks, I had a new best friend in the form of Amelia. We talked every day on the phone and spent lunch times together, plus we met up during the day between classes quite a bit. We couldn't really talk about boys together—after all, I could hardly go on about how hot her older brother was, but other than that, we were really comfortable around each other.

Nathan, on the other hand, seemed as uncomfortable around me as I was around him, so I was surprised when he sat next to me in art class one Friday afternoon. Tammie didn't take the class, and I liked to sit alone in the smaller section of the L shaped room because art was my favourite class with the only teacher who had ever encouraged me.

Her favourite piece of them was one which focused on a certain pair of eyes, so I was a little flustered when the owner of said eyes sat next to me before the class even began. Art was straight after lunch, so I tended to get in a little extra time by giving up some of my lunch. I was so focused that I didn't even hear the door opening.

"Hey, you busy?" Nathan said, coming up behind me.

"Erm, not exactly, you looking for Amelia? She should be in the lunch room."

"Yeah, I know. She told me you'd be here. I wanted to know if it would be okay if I joined you in this class. It's my weakest subject and the word is you're a bit of a prodigy, so maybe you could give me some tips or something? I'm not good with this whole thing," he said, waving his arms around vaguely.

"Oh."

He started to back away. "It's okay. You're busy. I'll see you later."

"No, no." I waved him back over. "It's cool. I was just surprised is all. Nobody cares about art around here apart from me." I tried to look as welcoming as possible while at the same time hide any of my artwork involving eyes that even slightly resembled his.

He sat down next to me and pulled a sheet of paper toward him. It was a rough sketch I had been working on of a dark forest which let in small shards of light between the trees.

"What's this?" he asked.

"This is going to sound stupid, I know, but my family have been talking about decorating and letting me do whatever with my room. I've always wanted to do a big mural behind my bed, so I figured I'd do my favourite sort of picture. Something like this. I like nature scenes, you know, forests and stuff? I don't know... it's just you can be alone but never completely alone, because there's so much life there."

"That's cool," he said.

"Not really. But it'll be mine, you know?"

He nodded, flicking through one of my old sketch pads. "You're really good."

"Not yet. But if I keep working at it then maybe one day I will be. Hopefully. It's the only thing I like so…" My voice trailed off as I realised I hadn't shut up talking since he sat down. He was a good listener though; he didn't interrupt.

I stiffened when I realised he had stopped at a sketch of a pair of eyes barely visible in a forest setting.

"What's this one about?" he asked, his face serious. I squirmed in my seat.

"Um, I have these dreams, so I sketch them. It's nothing. Just forget it."

He put the pad down and looked me straight in the eye, his expression so serious that my skin prickled in anticipation.

"I can't forget it. I have dreams too." He looked at me so seriously that I wasn't sure what to say. I didn't know exactly what he meant, and I was afraid to ask. I felt as though we were on the edge of something and about to jump off. I opened my mouth, but no words came out.

The art teacher breezed into the room at the right moment and chatted to us before setting up. By the time the bell rang and the rest of the class filtered into the room, we were back to being slightly comfortable.

Nathan had been right about one thing—he was really bad at art, drawing in particular. I couldn't resist teasing his exceptionally lame efforts.

"Hey, leave it out. We can't all be the secret love child of Picasso and Da Vinci." He looked at his artwork and sighed before crumpling it up.

"Ah, you're not completely hopeless," I told him. "You'll never be as good as me, obviously, but drawing is a skill. You can get better at it."

"Ha. Modest *and* beautiful. How *do* you keep your head from inflating?" he said with a good natured grin.

I looked at him sideways, not taking him seriously, but certainly feeling pleased with myself. We ended up talking for most of the double class. He told me about some of the places he had lived, and I oohed and aahed at the right parts. It was kind of hard to focus when I was so intent on staring at him, but I told him all about my favourite artists and some of the competitions I had entered. He was also good at oohing and aahing at the right parts.

It was amazingly easy to talk to Nathan when I wasn't worried about looking stupid in front of him or anyone else for that matter. Usually I had trouble looking people in the eye, but after a while, I was as comfortable with Nathan as I was with Amelia. I liked the sound of his voice, I liked how he looked, and I even liked how he smelled.

Apart from all that, he was a really decent person. Fun and witty, he wasn't mean, and he didn't badmouth anyone. I would have liked him even if he wasn't good looking—which made me feel better because I had been worrying about being shallow.

I ended up getting my hands plastered with paint as I re-worked one of my larger pieces. An annoyingly fuzzy lock of hair made its way out of my ponytail and decided to bounce around in front of my face. I blew at it ineffectively a few times before Nathan took pity on me.

Giving an exaggerated sigh, he brushed it back behind my ear, gently grazing my skin with his finger. Once again, I felt a spark of heat, almost like a shock of energy. I gave a little gasp.

"Shit," he muttered, pulling his hand back.

"Did you feel that too?" I asked in surprise. My ear felt like it had been held against a hot water bottle; it didn't hurt, but I could still feel the heat from his touch. There was something really odd about Nathan Evans.

Fear seemed to flit across his features, but then there was a new look on his face, something I'd never seen before. A flicker of emotion darkened his eyes, an element of wildness that gave me goose bumps. His pupils dilated all of a sudden, somehow making him look less human.

It was as if some mystery was slowly unravelling before my eyes. I was remembering something, kind of like déjà vu, but not exactly. I couldn't explain it because it wasn't like anything else I had ever experienced, but I *liked* how different everything was around Nathan.

He shook his head as if to gather his thoughts. He began to speak, his hand on my knee again, but Abbi interrupted him by sitting on the edge of the desk. Nathan hesitated, his cheeks flushed, then turned his back to me and spent the rest of the class flirting with Abbi.

More annoyed by the minute, every irritatingly false laugh cut through me. Grinding my teeth, I waited for the bell to ring. It dawned on me he had probably only sat with me because he thought I would do his work for him. *What a user!*

I left the room after class, before he even stood up, feeling disappointed. I had convinced myself he liked me back from the way he was acting, so weird and enigmatic yet lovely and charming. I probably wasn't even on his radar. I was setting myself up for a fall believing anything different.

"What's up?" Tammie said when we met up in the hallway before our next class.

"Nothing."

"Yeah. That's obvious. Come on, spill." She put her hands on her hips and refused to move.

"I don't know. I thought... I suppose I thought Nathan might like me or something. But he was just using me. I feel stupid now."

She frowned. "There's something a bit weird about those two, Perdy, I'm telling you. The more I see them, the more I dislike them."

"What, even Amelia?"

"Especially Amelia. I don't know why you're bothering with them at all, to be honest."

I couldn't hide my surprise. "Since when have you not liked them?"

"Ah, always. She's a total weirdo, Per. I dunno why you can't see it. As for him, don't waste your time. He's probably another Hannigan in the making. Hurry up, or we'll be late."

I followed her, stunned by her remarks. She had been as sweet as pie to Amelia for weeks. I couldn't believe I hadn't seen how she really felt.

After school, Tammie headed into town with her sister, while Joey stayed back for an advanced class. I walked to the bus stop with Amelia, surprised by how fond of her I was already. It felt like she was a long lost friend; she was so easy to be around compared to Tammie, who was always being negative about something or someone.

"Perdy, I've been wondering if you'd like to come to dinner at my house this weekend. Before you start, I've already said it to my family." Amelia gave me her puppy dog eyes look.

I would have said yes, but I didn't want to be around her brother. I couldn't say that, so I was willing to pretend everything was cool between Tammie and Amelia.

"Actually, I was going to ask you over to my place," I said. "Dad's working late this weekend, so I thought maybe you and Tammie and Joey could come over. I really don't want to be left on my own with those two at the moment."

She was about to speak when Nathan appeared beside her. He had a habit of seemingly emerging out of nowhere. I gave him one scornful glance, and then made a point of ignoring him completely. Amelia carried on talking as if nothing was wrong, but I couldn't bear him next to me. I said goodbye to her and her alone.

"Aren't you getting the bus with us?" she asked.

"Nah, I'd rather walk today. I'll call you later about this weekend."

I walked away, feeling a bit guilty for being so cold but knowing it had to be done. I couldn't stand next to someone who disliked me enough to use me when nobody else was around. The worst bit was I still liked him. Between the dreams and how I felt when we touched, one look from him was enough to make my stomach do a somersault. It was maddening. I had to keep away from that boy, for my own sake.

I was so annoyed that I almost didn't notice the woman standing across from the school in the exact same spot the red-haired man had been in. I wouldn't have paid any attention at all only it was beginning to seem a bit strange how all of these strangers were hanging around the school for no apparent reason.

She had long blonde hair that she almost hid behind, but I could still tell she was staring directly over at Nathan and Amelia who appeared to be in the middle of a hushed argument. I couldn't help watching the woman, wondering if they knew her, but she tensed up and looked directly at me. Even at that distance, I could feel the ice cold glare she aimed at me. I shuddered and kept moving, wondering what the hell her problem was.

Chapter Seven

Once again, I spent too much of my time thinking about Nathan Evans. I re-lived every time he spoke to me, looked at me, anything. I replayed conversations in my head to try and figure out if I was reading into them wrong. A part of me felt as though he liked me back. Another part of me thought he was playing a cruel game with me. He had acted really strangely about my dreams, almost as though he was admitting some shared experience with me. It was hard to tell for sure what exactly he had been trying to say in the art room.

Maybe he was just one of those boys who flirted with everyone. Who liked to charm random girls but had no real interest in them. Yet all those little things I experienced seemed to affect him too. I couldn't let go of the idea that there was something I didn't know about him, and that one thing would explain the rest. Or maybe I was even more pathetic than everyone assumed.

That weekend, Dad agreed to let me have my friends over and left Gran in charge. He had been making more of an effort, so I hugged him before he left for work. He wasn't the most tactile person in the world, but he hugged me back just as tightly, his way of clearing the air.

Joey, Tammie, and Amelia all turned up on Saturday afternoon. Gran went upstairs to give us a bit of space. Joey and Tammie decided to walk back to her house and look for a DVD to watch because nothing in my house was good enough, apparently.

Amelia and I shared some chocolate while we waited, content to flick through music stations until a song we both liked came on. From the corner of my eye, I could see her glance at me, twitching her foot incessantly. Finally I gave up and turned to face her.

"Okay, spit it out already."

She started to deny it, but thought better of it and nodded.

"All right, sorry, I know it's none of my business, but what's the deal with you and my brother? You seemed to be getting on okay, and then yesterday you blanked him completely. Plus, I got the feeling you were avoiding getting the bus or coming to my house because of him. Did you have a row? Or do you just not like him?" The look accompanying the last question plainly said that wasn't possible.

"There is no deal," I said, sounding as grumpy as I felt. "Besides, I can't talk to you about your brother."

"Of course you can! Who better to talk to than me?"

I wanted to blurt out everything in my head, but not to his sister; there was something gross about it. Worse still, there was always the chance she might think I made friends with her to get to him. Finally, I settled for shaking my head. "Just can't talk about it."

"But you like him, right?" she asked in a funny tone of voice, as if it was really important or something. I stared at her, wondering if I was that obvious. "You *do* like him."

"I can't talk about that stuff with you, Amelia," I said again.

She smiled, making me doubt she saw things the way I did. "It's okay Perdita. You can always talk to me. So, what did he do now?"

"He didn't do anything. Just leave it."

"I'm going to ask him if you don't tell me, so you might as well."

My mouth gaped open. The idea of her telling Nathan I was upset with him made me queasy. He would know I liked him, and that I was mad because I was jealous.

"You're so bloody pigheaded," I said, practically growling at her. "All right. I had a little bit of a crush on him, and I felt like... I don't know. I felt like he was leading me on a little bit, so I don't want to be around him anymore. That is all. End of story." I turned back to the television.

"But, how did he lead you on? What did he do? He can't lead you on if he likes you too."

I might have really pitied her if she wasn't annoying me so much. "Look, Amelia. I don't know what the story is with you; you seem to really want me and your brother to like each other, and that's sweet and all, but it isn't going to happen."

"But Perdita, you're meant to be. It's not because I want it. It's destiny. You like him, and he likes you."

I snorted. "Destiny? God, what are you like? Look. He doesn't like me, okay? He was a little bit flirty toward me, so I thought he might, but then he spent about half an hour yesterday with his back turned to me to chat up Abbi Mitchell, so no, he doesn't like me. And now I don't like him. Let's just stop now."

Her eyes grew wide with surprise. "That's not possible. I know for a fact he doesn't like Abbi Mitchell. He told me so."

"Well, maybe he lied. You're his sister, so why would he tell you things like that anyway? If he did like me, which he doesn't, then he would have said something. There's nothing stopping him."

"There is!" She gestured wildly.

"Like what?" My heart raced; could there really be a reason?

"He's..." She faltered. "He's a coward."

I shrugged, disappointed with the answer. "Who cares anyway? It's none of our business."

"I care! It's important! It's very, very important!"

I giggled, even though I was still annoyed. "Important?"

"Perdita, seriously! Please be honest with me for a minute, and I swear I'll leave it alone. Promise."

I nodded, willing to do anything to shut her up. Plus, I wanted to know why she was getting so agitated.

"Do you like him in a normal boy girl way, or does it feel way more intense than that, like, almost unnatural? Almost as if you already knew him or something? Like you've been waiting for him."

My cheeks flushed a deep red. No way was I answering that one truthfully. It sounded even weirder when someone else said it aloud. She knew exactly what I was feeling.

I cleared my throat. "Normal way."

To my surprise, she sat back in her seat with a huge grin on her face. "You're such a bad liar. I know for sure now. I know you'll end up together, and that's what matters."

She sounded so convinced that I almost believed her. But if Nathan liked me then surely he would have told me. He was confident and popular, so nothing could stop him—unless he was ashamed of me. My face burned at the likelihood of that thought. I was more than a little relieved when Gran came downstairs and stayed with us until Tammie and Joey returned empty-handed.

"I couldn't find anything, sorry. Nothing new anyway," Tammie said.

"Not unless you wanted to see The Notebook... *again*," Joey grumbled under his breath.

"So what'll we do now?" Amelia asked.

"Cinema?" Joey looked hopeful.

"You three go on. No chance of Dad letting me go." It wouldn't be the first time I'd missed out on something because of my Dad's rules.

Tammie and Joey exchanged guilty looks. I could tell they were trying to decide how long they could say no for before they went anyway, without seeming rude.

"Perdy, go," Gran said, pulling me aside.

"You know I can't."

"I'll take responsibility for it if he finds out. He won't ever know, but if he does, I'll take all the blame, I promise. If you go soon, then you'll be back before he finishes work. You deserve a little leeway. Go. Enjoy yourself."

I hesitated. I wanted to go out, but I was afraid of breaking the tentative trust between my Dad and me. When the others encouraged me, I caved and agreed. He might never find out. After all, he still didn't know that I ditched a couple of classes at school.

We looked in the papers to see what films were on that night. There was a choice between a soppy romance and a full on action thriller. We outvoted Tammie's romance by three to one. Action was definitely needed.

At the cinema, we wandered around the foyer to pass time, munching popcorn and sipping drinks out of oversized cups. Tammie groaned loudly, grabbing our attention.

"What's wrong?" Joey asked.

"Look who's here." She pointed toward the doors. A whole gang of people from our year filed in, among them Dawn, Aaron, and even Nathan. I glared at Amelia, but she shrugged.

"I swear I didn't know they would be here."

"Should we just go?" I said.

"Eh, no," Tammie said. "We already paid for our tickets. Besides, they're all in pairs, so they must be going to the other film. Lucky I was outvoted after all."

That was a small relief. I wouldn't have been able to relax if they had been behind us throwing popcorn and smart comments our way. I tried to quell the twinge of jealousy at seeing Nathan paired up with another girl. I prayed they wouldn't see us, but of course, they spotted us almost straight away. A sneer pulled up the corners of Dawn's mouth. She made sure we were looking at her before she put her arm around Nathan's waist.

Amelia gave a little snort and stood up. I prayed she was just going to the bathroom, but she walked straight over to Nathan.

"Oh, God, don't look," I hissed at Joey and Tammie. Of course they both looked over at Amelia, so I couldn't even pretend I was talking to them if anyone looked at *us*.

Nathan seemed surprised to see her and followed her over to the rest of us. I pretended I didn't see him at all. Childish, but effective. Until he said my name. Twice. "Hi," I said reluctantly.

"I didn't know you were coming out tonight," he said to nobody in particular.

"Last minute decision." Tammie tried to keep a straight face, but I caught the faux-sweet smile she sent in Dawn's direction.

"Yeah, we're going to see the action one," Joey added, oblivious to the awkward tension in the air.

"Really?" Aaron joined us. "They're making us see that lame chick flick. Here, Nathan, why don't we go with these instead? Let the girls see their chick flick without us getting forced into it."

"No!" I said, a little too loudly. "I just meant… that they couldn't ditch the girls is all."

"Oh, so it's like a date then?" Tammie piped up slyly.

Aaron laughed. "Nah, they just won the vote this time." He slapped his palm against Nathan's shoulder. "Come on, bud. We'll be bored stiff in there. At least, this way, we get to see what we want and still get the benefits after."

I felt like throwing up. Benefits? Nathan shrugged. "You can't just invite yourself along, Aaron."

"You go watch the chick-flick then. Joey doesn't mind if I tag along, do ya, Joey? I'll sit in between these two ladies," he said, gesturing toward Amelia and me with a creepy leer. We glanced at each other in mock horror behind his back.

"Maybe I'll tag along too then," Nathan said.

They went to get tickets and break the news to their friends. The other boys seemed disgusted they hadn't thought of the idea first, but they had already bought their tickets to the other film. It was almost worth sitting beside Aaron in the dark to see the look on Dawn's face. I couldn't help giggling.

"She's absolutely raging!" I whispered to Tammie. Tammie grinned. Anything that pissed off Dawn made her happy.

"Pity you and Amelia wouldn't go out with Nathan and Aaron. That would really sicken her," she whispered back. I gave her a filthy look in return.

We all took our seats before the trailers had even started. Tammie insisted we sit right at the back. She also made sure she and Joey sat next to each other. Amelia followed, but Aaron pushed past me to sit between us. Nathan sat on the other side of me. Amelia looked around Aaron with the most panicked look I had ever seen, so I bit the bullet and spoke to Nathan. I leaned in close, so I could whisper without Aaron hearing me.

"I'd swap with Amelia if I was you. So she doesn't have to sit beside *him*."

"What about you?"

"Who would you rather he sat next to? Me or your sister? Move."

His eyes softened, and for that second, I seriously believed Amelia had been right, and he really did like me.

"I've a better idea," he whispered back. "How about I swap with you and make out like I have to tell Aaron something, and then you could call Amelia over to you like you have something important to tell her. The lights will go out, and Amelia won't bother switching back."

"Evans, that is a fabulous idea."

"Rivers, I know."

He made a show of asking me to swap for a minute. While he distracted Aaron, I threw a piece of popcorn at Amelia and beckoned her over. She sat next to me, looking relieved.

"What's up?" she said.

"Your brother's idea," I said. "Want to sit next to him now?"

"No, thanks, you're both fine where you are," she said with a smirk. "Thanks by the way. I *so* didn't want to sit beside Aaron or those other two."

"Why not?"

"Something is definitely rumbling over there."

I glanced over at my cousin and friend and saw them sitting particularly close together.

The lights went down as the trailers started. Nathan leaned across me to ask if Amelia was okay. She nodded and waved him away, suspiciously engrossed by the ads. Nathan raised his eyebrows quizzically.

"Is she okay?" he whispered to me. I nodded in reply, still quite mad at him despite his brilliant plan.

"Are *you* okay?" he persisted. I glared back at him.

"Why are you mad at me?" he said, after a minute.

I could hardly tell him.

"Perdita?"

"I'm not mad," I hissed back.

"You look nice."

I shot him a nasty look. He ruined the effect by grinning back at me. I decided to ignore him. It was more difficult than I imagined. His arm tipped off mine so many times that it couldn't be accidental.

"Stop nudging me!"

"Stop ignoring me."

"I'm not!"

He turned in his seat to face me. "Why are you mad at me?"

"I'm not mad at you. I don't even know you. We're not friends, therefore, I cannot possibly be mad at you."

Even in the dark, I could see he was grinning at me. It was tremendously exasperating. Even more so when he leaned across me to speak to his sister.

"Amelia, why is *your* friend mad at me?"

She stared back at him. "Because *you're* a jerk."

He sat back in his chair with a sigh. I had completely lost the plot of the film by then.

"If I don't know what I'm doing to annoy you, then I can't stop doing it, can I? So tell me."

I heaved an aggravated sigh. "Okay, fine. You're acting like you're mentally unbalanced or something. One minute you act like you don't know me, next minute you act like we're friends, the next like we're… something else and then, oh, look, you're back to not knowing me again. I do *not* like it. So pick one, and leave me out of the rest. I don't appreciate being used to suit your mental mood swings." I sat back in my seat, sort of liberated I had said my piece, sort of mortified I had been so outspoken (for me) about it.

He was quiet for ages, so I figured he got the hint. But eventually, he leaned toward me again.

"I'm sorry, Perdita," he said, so softly I barely heard him. He patted my arm once or twice and then left me alone for the rest of the film. For some reason I was even more aware of his presence than before. Even when his hand was inches away from mine, my fingers pulsed and itched like they wanted to touch him.

I didn't have much experience with boys. None, actually. But he was complicated even for a boy. I didn't get him, nor did I understand his motives. He didn't act like anyone else I knew. I was completely and utterly confused and yet intrigued by him. Whatever he was playing at kept me interested. He looked at me like he was drawn to me too.

Nathan caught my eye and held my gaze a little too long. He leaned toward me, and for a split second, I felt sure he was going to kiss me. Before my heart even had the chance to race, I noticed people stirring in their seats. The end credits were rolling, and I hadn't watched fifteen minutes of the film. Nathan looked bewildered at the sudden movement and backed off, so I knew he hadn't been paying attention either.

"Great film," I said.

"Um, yeah, wasn't it? What was it about again?"

"No idea."

He grinned at me, and I couldn't help smiling back. Aaron stood and waited for us to move. Tammie and Joey still hadn't noticed the film was over, they were so absorbed in each other.

"Bucket of cold water," Amelia suggested, seeing my hesitation. "Only way they'll notice we're going."

Aaron solved the problem by clicking his fingers in front of their faces. They both blinked in surprise before it dawned on them the film was over. Looking sheepish, they followed us out. Our film had finished first, so it seemed polite to hang around with Aaron and Nathan while they waited for their friends. Nathan and I stood as close together as possible without actually touching.

Tension fissured the space between us every time he looked at me, but we didn't say a word.

The first batch of people finally trickled out of the screen-room. Among them was my father, holding the hand of a young blonde woman. I stepped toward him in shock, completely forgetting I was supposed to be at home.

"Dad?"

His whole face flushed red. "Uh, Perdy," he stuttered before getting his act together and becoming all Dad-like. "What are you doing here? I thought you were watching a film at home."

"And I thought you were working," I accused, hoping to deflect attention away from me. Dad glanced at his lady friend with guilty eyes.

"This is my friend, Erin. I, uh, I thought I was working tonight but they, uh, didn't need me in." His eyes darted around shiftily. His 'friend' held out her hand to shake mine.

"Hi, Erin. Dad, don't lie. Why didn't you just tell the truth?" I wasn't sure if I was icked out or amused by the whole thing.

"And what about trusting you to do the right thing?" he replied in a sterner tone.

Erin looked surprised. She had obviously only met nice, charming Dad. Now she was being introduced to the rule maniac.

"Gran gave me permission. Besides, I'm only at the cinema."

"With boys." He said it as though they were disease carrying monsters.

"Eh, no. Not with boys. I came with Joey, Tammie and Amelia, actually. Joey doesn't count as a boy. The others just happened to be at the cinema, too. They're only standing here waiting on their other friends. This is Amelia by the way. And that's her brother, so... so it's legit." My voice had risen a little with desperation. I didn't want to get into trouble in public.

Dad gave me a look that said who are you kidding, but he shook Amelia's hand nonetheless. He looked Nathan up and down a couple of times before he shook his. Nathan looked my father right in the eye and even spoke to him. I was majorly impressed, especially considering Aaron had run off and hidden in the toilets as soon as my Dad opened his mouth. Even Joey had backed away and half hidden himself behind a tall plastic fern.

"Sorry, sir. Perdita would be on her way home by now, but we wanted to wait until the others were finished so we could make sure everyone got home safely." Disgustingly smooth.

Most parents can't resist a responsible line about getting everyone home okay, and apparently, my Dad was no different.

"Oh, well, take your time then Perdy. Of course. Nathan, is it? I'm holding you responsible for everyone here. Well, uh, we're off. I'll see you at home later on, okay?" He gave me a quick hug before dragging Erin away. She waved goodbye to us all.

I whirled around to face Nathan. "What the hell did you do? Hypnotise him? Tammie, did you just see that? My Dad was all... reasonable!"

"Wow." Tammie looked impressed. "I've never seen anything like it. Perdy, he told you to take your time." She burst into fits of giggles. Amelia and Nathan didn't get it, but my Dad *never* said anything like that. Then again, he had never been reasoned with before either.

"Is he really that strict?" Nathan sounded doubtful.

"Um, understatement," Tammie scoffed.

"I'm not usually allowed out when it's dark or late or when he's working or, like, ever. My Gran persuaded me to go out tonight, so he didn't know. Usually he would flip out at something like that. He must have been trying to impress his lady friend," I said.

"Yeah, that was weird. Since when does your Dad go on dates?" Tammie made a face.

"Who knows? Wait until I tell Gran. I'm surprised he didn't beg me not to."

The others wandered over, and Dawn managed to find the time to throw me the evil eye. A perfect reminder of how things were meant to be.

"Anyway," I said, directly at Nathan but loud enough for the rest to hear. "We'll make sure Amelia gets home okay."

"Good idea," Dawn said, slithering up beside Nathan like she was going to lick him or something.

"Nah, I'll go with Amelia, once the rest of you are all back at home safe," he said.

"It's fine. Just do whatever you would have been doing if we didn't turn up; she'll be safe with us. Joey, Tammie, you ready?"

My friends gathered around me, half-heartedly saying goodbye to the others. Nathan hesitated for a few seconds before letting us go.

"Bus or taxi?" I asked outside.

"Taxi is safer," Joey said.

"Yeah, but the bus is cheaper," Tammie argued.

Tammie won. We got off near Amelia's house and stood outside her driveway until she went inside. I saw a dark haired man watch us from an upstairs window. Amelia's family were all kinds of strange.

As we walked to Tammie's house, my cousin and friend made eyes at each other, so I told them I was heading on by myself. They made an unenthusiastic attempt to stop me, but I insisted, so they went back to paying attention to each other.

I wasn't far from my own house. I had made the journey a million times. Not once had I been afraid. This was different. Something about the night kept the goose bumps raised on my arms. I instinctively looked behind me every few yards, convinced someone was there. I couldn't hear footsteps, but I didn't feel alone. The wind made strange whispers and howls; unexplainable shadows darted across my path, and my imagination ran wild.

Dark clouds swept across the moon. A streetlamp flickered on and off, unnerving me. Shivering, I crossed my arms, almost feeling as though I had to guard myself.

The walk seemed to last an eternity. My pace quickened along with my anxiety. A couple of times, I thought I heard a dog padding along behind me, but every time I looked around, there was nothing to be seen. I had my keys out before I even reached my house, but I worked myself up into such a panic that I couldn't fit the key in the lock.

My heart pounded in my ears, fooling me into hearing scarier noises. I pressed the doorbell urgently and backed up against the door, staring out into the dark. A black shadow in the distance seemed to bolt toward me. I fell backward as the door opened behind me.

I pushed against Gran and slammed the door behind us. Gripping her arm, I closed my eyes and released a long sigh of relief, feeling completely safe. Nothing was after me, and I was too old to get spooked by the dark.

"Are you okay?" She looked me over with concern.

I laughed out loud, feeling silly. "Oh, don't mind me. Just scaring myself. Is Dad back yet?"

"No, not yet. You're safe."

"He saw me already. You'll never guess what happened; he wasn't at work at all, and he was on a *date* in the cinema with some woman."

"Really? Was she pretty?"

"Yeah, actually," I said, remembering. "Pretty, young, blonde. Hey, is Dad going through a mid-life crisis?"

I forgot all about how scared I had been outside as I scandalised my grandmother with tales of my straitlaced Dad's deceit. We tried to wait up for him to get some gossip, but he stayed out too late, and we were already tired. Before I went to bed, I glanced out of the window and was almost certain I saw a huge dog run up the road. Except it was so big, I found it hard to believe it was just a dog. I stayed at the window for ages hoping to see it again.

That night, I dreamt that a gang of gigantic, wild dogs were chasing me, but a boy with lovely brown eyes came and sent them away. As far as dreams went, it wasn't too bad.

Chapter Eight

The next morning, I got up bright and early, feeling thoroughly refreshed. I went outside to get our Sunday papers while Gran and Dad finished their breakfast. Instead of the papers, I found something else. I gave a little shriek that sent Dad and Gran running outside after me. A dead tabby cat, its eyes wide open and glazed over, lay on our doorstep.

"Sorry," I said. "I just got a fright."

"Oh, the poor thing," Gran said. "It must have lain there to die during the night."

Dad leaned over, his forehead creasing into a deep frown as he peered at the cat. Straightening his back, he nudged the cat with his foot. A slight movement was all it took for me to realise it hadn't picked our doorstep to die on. Before Dad could push us back inside, I saw the animal's insides spill out from the gaping hole in its torso. Blood drops trailed from our gate to our front door. Feeling sick, I backed into the house with Gran, who was more than a little shaken judging by the paleness of her cheeks. I made her a cup of coffee while Dad disposed of the body and cleaned up outside.

"What happened to it?" Gran asked when he came back inside.

His face was grim. "It looks like some sort of animal ripped open its stomach and then carried it to our door, for some reason. I don't know how it did it so neatly."

"Could a dog have done it?" I said, thinking hard. "I thought I saw a dog outside last night."

"Maybe," he conceded as he scrubbed his hands. "Still seems strange. Why carry it here and then leave it? And so carefully. Bizarre."

"Poor kitty," I said sorrowfully.

"Do you still want a dog after this?" Dad said.

"Yeah. But we should rescue a kitten too."

"Don't push your luck. Especially after last night."

Gran almost crowed with excitement, immediately distracted. I tried my hardest to force the image of the slaughtered cat out of my mind, but I wasn't as easily side-tracked as my grandmother.

"Oh, yes, last night. How was work?" she teased.

Dad's face turned pink. "Aw, leave him alone, Gran," I said, forcing a smile. "But you won't get away with not telling us anything, so you better spill, Dad."

He rolled his eyes, knowing full well we would gang up on him all day if he didn't talk.

"Okay, okay! I lied about having to work. Erin is a medical secretary in the hospital, and we decided to go to the pictures together. As friends. Perfectly normal. No big deal."

"I don't hold hands with my friends. Grandmother, do you?"

She shook her head in mock seriousness. "No, granddaughter, I don't."

"Oh, stop it." Dad tried to sound stern, but I could hear the laughter in his voice. "And you're one to talk Perdy. You just happened to bump into Amelia's brother last night?"

"Eh, yeah actually!" I said as indignantly as I could manage.

"Amelia's brother?" Gran's eyes gleamed with this new piece of information.

"Don't turn it around on me, Dad! What were we supposed to say? No Amelia, your brother can't be seen with us? Pfft."

Dad laughed heartily, a rarity in our house. Gran and I glanced at each in bemusement. He hadn't given me any grief for going out without his permission. Maybe this Erin woman was a good influence on him. I wasn't sure if I liked the idea of him having a girlfriend, but if it helped him lighten up then I had no problem reaping the benefits.

As soon as Gran left the room, I grabbed the opportunity to ask Dad about the cat. I couldn't stop thinking about it.

"Do you really think a stray dog did that?"

"Of course."

"It just seems weird. Maybe some sicko could have done it?" I wasn't sure why that thought was in my head, but lately, I hadn't felt as safe as usual.

Dad smiled. "Don't be so melodramatic, Perdy. I know you're upset, but keep that imagination under control. Your Gran told me how scared you were last night when you came in. Besides, you said yourself you thought you saw a dog."

I scowled. I *had* been silly the night before, but it didn't mean he should discount my opinions straight off.

"Come on, Perdy, cheer up. It was just a one-off."

Something about the whole thing didn't sit right with me. I couldn't pinpoint exactly what, so I smiled back at Dad and tried to forget about it.

Gran went out that afternoon, leaving Dad and me at home. I figured it would be nice to spend some time together for a change.

"Hey Dad, wanna watch a DVD with me? I'll let you pick. I won't even hide the Jean-Claude Van Damme DVDs this time."

Dad cleared his throat and fidgeted with his watch. "Actually, I have plans with Erin today. Why don't you go over to Tammie's house or something?"

My face fell. The one day I didn't want to be alone. I straightened photo frames on the mantelpiece to distract myself.

"Erin? Again? What's the story with you two, Dad?" I pinched my bottom lip with my teeth in an effort to keep my face expressionless.

"It's no big deal. Is it?"

He met my eyes, and for the first time, I saw him looking for my permission or blessing or some sign I wouldn't make things awkward for him. Since my mother left him, he had put me and his job before personal relationships. Deep down, I knew it wouldn't be fair to ruin his chances now.

"You're the only one who knows if it's a big deal or not, but in my opinion, it's about time you had some fun. You were getting a little boring there for a while, you know."

His face lit up. It reminded me of when I was younger, before Dad had started worrying about boys or alcohol or failing in school. He had always been protective, but once upon a time, he had also fun to be around. If he rediscovered that side of himself with Erin, then who was I to interfere? Still, when he left I felt completely alone. It was surprisingly hard to shake that left behind feeling.

I tried to paint, but after staring at a blank canvas for twenty minutes, I decided to give up on that idea. I turned to cleaning to distract myself. I worked on scrubbing away the niggling fears in the back of mind. No more murdered cats, staring strangers, and brown-eyed boys.

Tammie popped around for a while to make sure I had gotten home okay.

"Well, if I hadn't, it'd be a bit late now to check up on me," I said, mopping the kitchen floor aggressively.

"As if anything could happen to you five minutes away from your house," she scoffed. "Stop cleaning. Why are you cleaning?"

I rolled my eyes and put everything away. "So?" I said when I sat down next to her.

"So, what?"

"Little Miss Innocent today? So, what's going on with you and Joey?"

"Nothing, why?" she said, but she was grinning from ear to ear.

"Tammie...."

"Seriously, nothing happened. We flirted a bit, which was a nice change, but he didn't do anything or try anything or say anything important."

"Disappointed?"

She stretched her arms out behind her head. "Nah. Progress is progress and all that."

"Looked like progress, all right. We were all afraid to sit next to you in the cinema."

"But do you think he'll make a move soon?" she said, her forehead creasing with worry.

"No, Tammie. I told you before. You'll have to make the first move. You know what he's like."

"What about you and the Evans chap?"

I felt like getting the mop out again. "What about me and... him?"

"Anything interesting happen?"

"Ha. Yeah, right."

"You sat next to each other."

"So? Amelia sat on the other side of me, and you're not asking about me and her."

Tammie laughed. "The lady doth protest too much. Are *you* disappointed then?"

"No. I know better than to expect anything." I smiled at her. "Dad was morto this morning by the way."

She chuckled with unbridled glee. "Oh, yeah! Who would have thought Old Man Rivers would be getting more action than you? Oh, the shame!"

"Shut up! Anyway, have you heard from my cousin today?"

She shook her head. "I might knock over to him."

"Alone?"

She avoided my eyes. "Well, maybe."

"It's cool. Go on. You might want to do something about your hair though."

She touched her fringe, horrified at the thought there was something wrong with it.

"I'm kidding!" I said, laughing. "Go on, I'll meet you at the bus stop in the morning."

When she left, the house felt empty. Lonely. It was only a matter of time before Tammie and Joey started going out together. I figured I should get used to it.

The landline rang; I answered, hoping it was Tammie, but nobody said a word. I heard breathing, so I said hello a couple of times before hanging up and putting it down to a wrong number. Maybe I was still freaked out over the dead cat, but I couldn't ignore the cold feeling in my gut when I put down the phone.

I wandered around the house not really knowing what to do. I was so grateful when my mobile rang that I raced up the stairs to answer it.

"Hello?" I said, panting a little.

"Perdy? You okay?"

"Oh, hey Amelia. Yeah, I just ran up the stairs to get the phone. How are you?"

"Good, thanks. Any news on Tammie and Joey?"

"She popped over for a minute. She's gone to his house now, working on it. She reckons she's getting there."

"Ah, good. So, what are you doing?" She sounded chirpy enough to turn my mood around.

"Em, nothing really. On my own here. You?"

"Nothing either. Wanna come over?"

I hesitated. I wasn't sure I wanted to go over if Nathan was around. Being honest, I wasn't sure I wanted to go over if he wasn't.

"I don't know," I said.

"It's okay. You don't have to be shy or anything. If you don't want to see... anyone in particular then we can hide out in my room."

I couldn't help smiling. "I'll just ring my Gran and ask is it okay first, yeah?"

"Sure, see you."

It was pretty sly of me to ask Gran, knowing my Dad would say no. She agreed readily when I asked if I could go. She even told me to stay for dinner if I was invited. I rang Amelia again; she told me to hurry up. I took a couple of minutes to stress out about meeting Amelia's family, and a little part of me was afraid to go outside at all, but I put it to the back of my mind.

Before I even made it to her door, Amelia ran out to greet me, followed by a huge grey dog. It was almost as big as the one I'd seen outside my house. It walked straight up to me and nuzzled my hand.

"What's this? A horse?"

"No, one of our dogs, King. Isn't he handsome?" she enthused.

He was a bit scruffy looking, but he had beautiful, loyal, trusting eyes that reminded me of Dolly.

"He's pretty nice, all right," I said, giving the dog a scratch behind his ears. He whined appreciatively. His hair was shaggy, sort of wiry, but he was well groomed. I was used to Dolly being bouncy and hyper, so this calm giant didn't intimidate me at all. When I stopped giving him attention, he nudged me repeatedly.

"Okay, you're more than nice," I told him. "What did you say he is? A wolfhound?"

"Yep. He's my favourite."

"He seems to like you."

I looked around to see who was speaking. A tall, broad man, who looked remarkably like Nathan, except with curly hair and a slightly darker shade of skin, approached us. The same man I had spotted watching us the night before. A shiver ran down my spine when he looked at me.

"This is my uncle, Byron," Amelia said, tugging him by the arm.

"Nice to meet you," I said. He didn't hold his hand out to be shaken.

"He doesn't usually like strangers," he said, nodding at King. Byron's voice was rich and deep, but his eyes were cold, almost completely devoid of emotion. Even though Amelia clung to him, he didn't respond in any way.

"Lucky me." I wasn't sure what to make of Byron. He seemed so stern and aloof.

"Indeed. Amelia, take her inside to meet your grandmother. She's waiting in the kitchen."

Amelia linked my arm and led me into the house, chatting away excitedly. King padded after us. I looked behind me to see Byron standing very still, watching us intently.

"Where are your other dogs?" I whispered, trying to forget about her strange uncle.

"You don't have to whisper," she whispered back. "They're out with my grandfather and Nathan. King always stays with me."

The house surprised me. It was so modern compared to the outside. The part that really caught my attention was the hallway because it was covered in photos and paintings of wolves. Most people I knew had pictures of their families on their walls. The effect was unsettling. Goosebumps covered my arms as I realised the large dog I had seen outside my house looked an awful lot like a wolf.

In the kitchen, Amelia's grandmother hugged me tight, as if I was a long-lost relative. Her hair was almost white, and she had plenty of wrinkles, but her bone structure was amazing, so she looked much younger than my Gran. Her skin was a dark mocha colour, and she smelled nice and fresh, sort of like violets. She was the opposite of the reserved Byron, so warm and friendly, that it was easy to see where Amelia got it from.

"It's so nice to meet you, Perdita," she said. Her accent was also mixed, but I caught hints of a French accent in there. "You're welcome here anytime."

"Mémère, look at King. He's following Perdita around." Amelia pointed at the dog who nudged my hand with his nose, trying to get my attention.

"King, out." Amelia's grandmother shooed him away.

"It's okay, Mrs. Evans," I said.

"Mrs. Evans, how sweet. Amelia was named for me, but you may call me Lia, if you like." Lia looked at me a little too long. Now I knew where Amelia got it from.

"Oh. Right. Thanks. Uh, Lia." I felt awkward all of a sudden, but she led me into the room, her arm around my shoulders.

"Sit down while I make a snack for everyone. Opa will be back soon. Amelia, pour yourself and Perdita a glass of juice while you wait for him."

We sat at the dining table with our drinks while Lia prepared a snack. The snack turned out to be huge omelettes filled with pretty much the entire contents of their fridge. She took the last of the mixture from the frying pan as Nathan walked in, his forehead streaked with muck. Four more dogs traipsed in but were ordered back outside by Amelia. As soon as Nathan saw me, he stopped in his tracks. He barely said hello before he backed out of the room. I wasn't even a little bit surprised.

"I'll be right back," Lia said, her smile never reaching her eyes. "Amelia, could you begin to serve the food, please?"

An elderly man strode in, his back perfectly straight, and kissed Amelia on the forehead.

"This is my grandfather, Perdita," she said, her voice prouder than ever. "Opa, *this* is Perdita."

Amelia's grandfather beamed at me. He took my hand and held it between both of his large ones, shaking it gently.

"Ah, I didn't know you would arrive today. Welcome to our home. We're all delighted to meet you." His voice was still heavy with more than a trace of a German accent, and his eyes twinkled as he spoke.

Mr. Evans, or Jakob, as he told me to call him, sat next to me. He pushed King out of his way and chatted easily to me. I couldn't feel shy around him.

Amelia set large plates full of food in front of us and sat on the other side of me. They both tucked in and encouraged me to join them. The portion on my plate was a similar size to Amelia's, but I couldn't imagine eating it all. The rest of the plates had double portions. I couldn't understand how they were all so lean. Lia and Jakob were in much better shape than my Dad, never mind my Gran.

Lia came back into the room followed by Byron and the now clean Nathan. Lia and Jakob carried the conversation. I was happy to eat and listen. It was strange to sit there with another family. My family rarely ate together, and even when we did, we didn't exactly chat like Amelia and her grandparents.

Lia and Jakob clearly idolised Amelia. They hung on to her every word and looked at her as if she was their most precious possession. I could see why she was so upset when anyone was mean to her; she hadn't heard a bad word at home. Byron ate quickly and excused himself, saying he had to work. He was another Evans male who was hard to figure out.

"He works very hard," Lia said to me, as if to excuse him. He wasn't rude or anything, but the contrast between himself and his own parents was dramatic.

"So, Perdita, you are in the same year as Nathan, yes?" Jakob asked me.

I nodded. Jakob seemed delighted.

"And what is he really like in class?" he said.

"Same as right now, really," I replied. They all chuckled except for Nathan who lifted his head to glare at me.

"And my granddaughter, is she as bratty as her brother likes to make out?"

I shook my head. "Not even a little bit. She acts like, well, you and your wife pretty much."

Jakob seemed pleased with that answer. "Ah, I must thank you, too. For making sure my girl came home safely last night."

"No problem. It's pretty safe around here though."

"That's partly why we decided to move here," Lia informed me. "Amelia tells us you live with your grandmother, too?"

"Yeah, and my Dad."

"He is a doctor, yes?" Jakob said.

"Yes. He works in the local hospital."

"Enough questions," Amelia said, yawning with boredom. "Can't we go listen to music or something?"

"*You* can't. It's your turn to wash up," Lia reminded her.

"I'll help," I offered.

"No, guests don't help! Nathan, take Perdita into the living room while she waits for Amelia, please," Lia said.

He hesitated long enough for me to expect him to refuse, but he eventually stood up and gestured for me to follow. It was as if he was grumpy that I was in his home. I was starting to think he was pretty rude. Yet again, he had done a complete one-eighty compared to the night before.

The living room was large and bright, not much furniture, but what was there was attractive yet comfortable looking. They had a huge flat screen television on the wall. Nathan picked up a remote and stood there, flicking through channels.

"Sit anywhere," he said. I chose the corner of a large sofa. It was squishier than it looked. He sat at the other end of the same chair, still messing with the television. It was altogether too awkward. I opened and closed a button on my cardigan repeatedly, not quite knowing what to do. I prayed that Amelia would hurry up, but she took ages. We sat in silence for so long that I wondered if he had an evil twin who kept charming me.

"Did Joey walk you home last night?"

I shook my head. "I left them at Tammie's."

"They should have walked you."

I shrugged. I *had* gotten a bit freaked out the night before while I was alone, but that was a one off. I didn't need to be walked to my door because of it.

"You don't have to sit here, you know," I told him. His cheeks flushed a little.

"I don't mind."

I smiled at that. He was right on the edge of the chair, fidgeting. The epitome of the word uncomfortable.

"Yeah, I can see that," I said. He looked down at himself and made a visible effort to relax.

"Sorry," he blurted out. "It's just… weird seeing you here. I didn't know you were coming over."

"Amelia rang me and asked me to come over because I was at home alone. She said we'd stay in her room, so I said okay. Sorry to, like, disturb you and all."

He raised his hands in protest. "No, that's not what I meant. I was just surprised. Nothing bad."

"Yeah, sure," I said, rolling my eyes.

As soon as Amelia came to get me, Nathan disappeared. Amelia and I headed outside to a pair of old swings in the long back garden. King followed us out and sat close to us. The fences around the neighbouring gardens were all gone so there was one huge strip of land outside their home. As all of the other houses were empty, Amelia's family had it all to themselves.

"This is kind of cool," I told her, swinging like a little kid. "All of this space to yourselves."

"It's more creepy than cool," she admitted. "Especially at night."

"Your brother doesn't seem impressed that I'm here," I said, hoping she would contradict me.

"Don't mind him, he's always grumpy," she said.

I lay back and watched the clouds, swinging gently all the time. I forgot Amelia was there and started humming to myself.

"Here he is now," Amelia said, and I jerked upright with a fright, grabbing the rope to help keep my balance. Nathan approached us almost sheepishly, his hands in his pockets. He stood by Amelia's swing and looked at the sleeping dog on the ground next to me.

"What do you want?" Amelia said tartly.

He shrugged. "King," he called. King opened one sleepy eye and then completely ignored Nathan.

"What a great dog," I said with a smile and began to swing again.

"Stupid animal." Nathan shook his head. "He's supposed to be a guard dog, and he goes asleep at a stranger's feet."

"Dogs are a better judge of character than humans are, I'll have you know," I said.

Amelia stuck her tongue out at Nathan. "She's not a stranger, Nathan. You know that better than anyone."

A flash of anger clouded Nathan's features but passed just as quickly. Amelia gave him a strange, smug look. Once again, I felt as though I was missing something.

"Yeah, well, Cúchulainnn wouldn't be that easy to get by."

Out of nowhere he put his little fingers in his mouth and whistled loudly. I jumped in fright, almost falling off the swing.

"What the hell? Warn people before you do that right next to them!"

"Sorry," he said, laughing as something came racing toward us with a bark. Cúchulainnn turned out to be another wolfhound, even larger than King. This one was fawn coloured, a beautiful looking dog with eyes that were wilder than King's. He watched me warily for a few seconds. Sniffing the air, he stalked over to me and let me pet him. Nathan's eyes widened in surprise.

"Did that just happen?" he asked Amelia who was in a fit of laughter at his face. "What are you doing to my dogs?" he said to me, but he looked kind of pleased.

"They're just clever puppies. Aren't you Cúchulainn? Oh, yes, you are," I gushed. "Great name by the way."

"Our grandparents lived in Ireland before. They like the old myths and legends," Amelia said.

"Hit me. See what he does." Nathan came closer and patted his jaw.

"Nathan!" Amelia sounded horrified.

"I won't let him hurt her. I just want to see what he does."

I moved my arm to thump his while he was distracted by Amelia, but he grabbed my wrist without even looking around.

"Ouch," I hissed. Cúchulainn gave a low growl, but he wasn't directing it at me. He was warning Nathan to let go.

"Sorry," he said, quickly letting go of my wrist. "I didn't mean to do that."

As soon as he let go, Cúchulainn settled down again. Nathan stared at me as if I was a complete freak of nature. Amelia jumped off her swing.

"I have to tell Opa about Cúchulainn. He'll never believe me!"

She ran toward the house, looking as if she might burst with excitement. I rubbed my wrist absent-mindedly, wondering how he had caught my arm so quickly without looking.

"Are you okay?" Nathan asked in concern. "I'm sorry. I can't get used to…" His voice trailed off.

"Used to what?" I asked, curious.

"Nothing. I just… I really didn't mean to grab you. It was reflexes or something."

"It's fine."

Nathan took my arm, gently this time. He peered at the tiny red mark with a worried look on his face.

"Seriously, it's fine now," I reassured him. He stroked the inside of my wrist with his thumb, all the while looking from me to his dogs.

"That was too weird," he said. "He's never acted like that with me before."

"He just got a fright or something. Joey's dog gets all jumpy whenever Tammie laughs. Um… Nathan?" I gestured toward my wrist with my free hand.

"Oh. Sorry," he said, letting go. He clenched his fists, stretching out his fingers and then closing them again. "I'm glad you came over," he said at last. "Even if you did turn my dogs against me."

Amelia returned with her grandparents. Lia scolded Nathan for wanting to test out the dog's reactions on me, but she didn't sound surprised at all.

"I warned you," she said under her breath, but I heard her.

A family row seemed to be building up, so I cleared my throat and told them I should get going.

They turned their attention to me then, all except Nathan, who seemed quite relieved. I explained why I had to go, but they didn't seem to get it.

"He's really strict, Opa. She'll get into trouble if she stays," Nathan said at last.

"Okay," Jakob conceded. "But Nathan will walk you home. I would not like my girl walking the streets alone."

"It's okay; it's safe here. I promise, there's no need for anyone to take me home." I didn't know whether to be embarrassed or annoyed by how little confidence adults had in my ability to take care of myself.

"It's all right," Nathan said. "I'll take Cúchulainn with me for a walk. He needs the exercise. It's no hassle, Perdita."

They all insisted then. I found it difficult to say no to so many people at the same time, so I ended up agreeing just to make them happy.

"Don't worry," Nathan whispered to me as we left. "If you want me to go, then I will, but they won't let you leave until they get their own way. Trust me." I nodded, waving goodbye to the others. Nathan had Cúchulainn on a lead, but the dog was so big that I didn't think a lead would stop him if he decided to run off.

"I'm bringing him for a walk anyway, so I might as well see you home," Nathan said after a moment of silence. "If you really don't want me to, I can go a different way, but it's no problem for me, okay?"

I nodded; even though he blew hot and cold, I liked being around him, so I wasn't going to remind him he had already taken the dog for a walk. Cúchulainn sniffed at everything, but he was pretty obedient. He didn't even pull on the lead.

"I want my dog to be like that," I said, half to myself.

"Like what?"

"Well-trained like that. He's very good."

"Are you getting a dog?"

"Maybe. Joey's dog is supposed to be having a litter. They said I can have one."

"I could help you train it if you liked."

That made me smile. "Thanks, but you'll probably be gone by the time I have a dog."

"Why's that?"

"Oh," I said, blushing. "I just meant that you move around a lot, so Amelia said, and Dolly may not even be expecting this time, so you might have moved on by the time she has a pup."

"We're not planning on moving, but if we're here—and you want help, that is—I could show you some stuff. Give you tips or something. Whenever."

"Oh, okay. Thanks."

Cúchulainn acted up as we passed the woods. The hackles on the back of his neck stood up, and he gave a low growl. I looked around and frowned, seeing an all too familiar red-haired figure across the road, walking in the opposite direction. If I didn't know better, I would think the man was following me. Nathan nudged me. Distracted, I realised he had been speaking to me.

"Sorry, what?"

"I said, it was probably just a rabbit or mouse or something."

"Oh, right, poor mouse wouldn't stand a chance against your monster dog."

"Wolfhounds aren't really aggressive. Just tall."

"I've seen taller," I said, remembering the night before.

"Yeah, right," he scoffed.

"Really. Last night, I saw a huge scruffy thing outside my house. Looked way bigger than Cúchulainn here."

Nathan frowned. "That's odd."

"Not really," I said, but my gut was clenched with tension because a whole lot of things felt odd to me.

Cúchulainn gave a little yelp and dashed off, pulling Nathan around in a circle. I tried not to laugh as he untangled himself from the lead. He swore at the dog, but his laughter ruined the effect.

"So, are you going to the party next weekend?" he asked.

"Erm, I don't usually get invited to parties," I said with a small laugh.

"Oh," he said, frowning. "I'm pretty sure Aaron said he was going to invite you."

"Aaron? We're not friends."

"So? Maybe he likes you. Is that a bad thing?" He looked at me with an interest that confused me.

"Aaron Hannigan doesn't like girls. He likes trying to get girls to like him. And he is so not interested in me. Never has been, never will be, and vice versa."

Nathan smiled. "So you're best buddies then."

"I don't think you get what things are like around here. If he's nice to me, it's because I'm friends with your sister. That's all. He would have never been caught dead in the cinema with any of us before you arrived."

"Why?"

"Because we're the freaks. We're not popular. Get it?" I laughed.

"Well, I think you're cool," he said with a wink.

"You have to be nice to your little sister's friend. Or she'll rat on you," I teased.

"I'm not scared of her. She *is* a bit of a brat by the way."

I smacked his arm. "She is not! She's lovely."

He grabbed my waist and squeezed, managing to get a ticklish part. I squirmed away, laughing. He reached for me again, but I skipped out of his way.

For an instant, I forgot all about the way he sometimes acted and enjoyed being around him. When it was just us, everything was cool.

As if she could sense my momentary happiness, Dawn turned the corner ahead of us, accompanied by Abbi. I couldn't help groaning. Nathan grinned at me in amusement. Dawn hurried toward us when she saw him, managing to give me one of her trademark sneers along the way.

"Hey, Nate," she said, overly chirpy. She was never like that when he wasn't around. "Whatcha doing? Babysitting?"

I scowled at her, but it slid off my face as soon as Nathan casually draped his arm around my shoulder. Abbi tried not to laugh.

"What are you on about, Dawn?" I wasn't sure what Nathan was playing at, but Dawn was obviously not impressed. Her hands on her hips, she looked me up and down in disgust.

"Whatever you're into," she said as snidely as she could manage. Then she snapped out of it and beamed at Nathan. "I think I'm the one who needs to be walked home by you after everything I've gone through today."

"What do you mean?" he asked.

"I headed out to meet Abbi and, get this, there was a dead rabbit in my garden!" She paused for dramatic effect.

Nathan glanced at me, but my heart had started pounding. "Okay?"

"I don't mean just dead. I mean, like, its head was ripped clean off. So disgusting. I'm literally traumatised for life."

Nathan made a face. "Yuck. Maybe it was a fox or something."

"Don't say that," she exclaimed. "I'll never be able to sleep knowing there are wild animal outside." She opened her eyes as wide as possible. "My life could be in danger!"

Abbi rolled her eyes and moved on, dragging a resistant Dawn after her. A low growl rumbled in Cúchulainn's throat. Dawn edged backward, her eyes widening as she tried to swallow her panic. Nathan let Cúchulainn take one step toward her. That was all it took. Dawn shrieked and tripped over herself in her hurry to get away.

"See you two at school," Abbi said with a wink. "Don't do anything I wouldn't do," she added before hurrying after Dawn.

Nathan didn't even wait until we were out of earshot to start laughing.

"Eh, what's all this about?" I said, pointing at his arm which was still around me.

"Sorry," he said, distancing himself. "She's just so annoying. All she does is say horrible things, and she can't take no for an answer. She drives me mad, so I thought I'd do the same to her. Was that mean?"

"A bit."

He laughed again. "Good. She's awful."

I felt disappointed he used me to get his own back at someone.

"You seem a lot more cheerful now," I said.

"People depress me," he said, his mood suddenly switching again. I raised an eyebrow. "Not you, but sometimes that house,"—he shook his head—"My family can be a bit much sometimes, you know? They expect me to be a certain way, and I can't. It's like everyone wants me to be something I'm not."

"I get it. Mine can make me feel like my head is going to explode."

"Yeah, same here. I can't be myself around them. I always feel like I'm playing a part or something."

That hit me hard. It was exactly how I felt most of the time. "I know what you mean. I wish they'd let me be me, or at least let me find out who me is," I said. "They're so busy trying to make me like them that they can't see anything else."

"Exactly," he said. "I don't even know you properly, and you get me better than they do. Better than anyone does."

I had to laugh. "I don't think I get you very often. You confuse me more than anyone else."

He glanced at me to see if I was serious. "You look at me as if you know me," he said, hesitant.

"Do I?" I bowed my head, feeling shy.

"You do. Sometimes I'm afraid you know all my secrets."

I grinned up at him. "Are they that bad?"

"Depends on who you ask."

"They can't be that bad."

"Maybe they would shock you. Scare you even." He didn't smile.

I studied him for a moment, running my mind over the worst possible things I could think of. "I don't think so. If your big ass dog didn't scare me…"

He smiled. "I wish I could tell you all my secrets so."

"Nobody's stopping you."

"Ah. Except for me," he said in a curiously sad tone of voice.

"Well, you're the only boss of you," I said, trying to sound light-hearted. "I live over there." I pointed to my house.

"That was quick. I guess I should probably leave you here in case your Dad is home, yeah?"

I nodded. "Thanks, but yeah, exactly. Thank you for walking me home."

"My pleasure." He bit his lip. "I better go. See you tomorrow?"

"I suppose so," I said, but I waited. He lingered for a few seconds, as if he didn't want to leave, but his dog seemed eager to follow a scent, so he waved goodbye. As soon as he walked away my mood bottomed out.

Gran ambushed me as soon as I walked in the door. She was one of those nosy neighbours who spend way too much time peering through curtains in case they miss something.

"Was that Amelia's brother? Isn't he a cute one! I always knew you had good taste."

"Gran, don't. I'm not in the mood for your teasing. His grandparents made him walk me home. That's all."

She raised an eyebrow.

"Really, Gran," I said, a little upset because I was actually telling the truth.

Gran hugged me and said nice, reassuring things until I smiled. We sat down together and had a chat about what was going on in my life. I didn't tell her how often I thought about Nathan, or the fact I dreamt about him all time, or even how much better I felt whenever I was close to him.

I did tell her how Tammie and Joey seemed to be getting closer, and I felt left out. How Amelia was trying to push me and Nathan together, but it wasn't working. I even admitted how much I liked him, and how hurt I was when he kept playing hot and cold with me.

"Ah, mo ghrá. Didn't I ever tell you that's how teenage boys are?"

I shook my head, feeling sorry for myself.

She smiled at me. "You know, I remember your mother crying in my arms when she wasn't much older than you because your Daddy laughed at her in front of everyone. When they were alone, he acted like he loved her, but when his friends were around, oh, he was awful to her."

"Really? My Dad did that?"

"Of course he did. He was a teenage boy, wasn't he? They take longer to mature. Girls know what they want years before boys ever do."

That made me laugh. I couldn't imagine my Dad being immature. "So what did you tell her?"

"I said, give him a few months, and he'll be the one following you around. And he was! She played it cool, of course. Then he practically camped outside our door. Your grandfather wasn't impressed. He didn't think she was old enough for a boyfriend, and he thought your father was too old because he was already in college. Your grandfather was a strict man."

"Was he?"

"Oh, yes. He wouldn't let Stephen into the house, and he forbade your mother from seeing him. Of course, that had the opposite effect. She liked him all the better for standing up to your grandfather. She started sneaking out to see him. Her father went crazy. He even locked her in her room."

My eyes grew wide. I didn't know any of this. "And what happened then?"

My Gran's eyes dimmed as she remembered. "She didn't come home from school one day. We were mad with worry. We didn't know what was happening until she rang us to say they had eloped, and they weren't coming back."

"Wow. That was awful."

Gran nodded. "Your grandfather… well, he wasn't the same after that. He was heartbroken because she had been his little pet all of her life. She refused to visit, rarely contacted us at all. Eighteen months later, he had a heart attack and died. She turned up shortly after the funeral. You were with her. Just a tiny baby. I didn't even know I was a grandmother until then. Your father had stayed behind. He couldn't miss his classes. We had a lovely few days together. Like the old days again. Then I woke up one morning, and you were screaming your head off for a feed. She was gone."

I squeezed Gran's hand. Her eyes had misted over. She cleared her throat and carried on, as if she had to finish the story.

"She rang me the next day to tell me she couldn't cope with being married. Being a mother. She wanted her own chance at life. She wanted to go back to school and be somebody." Gran laughed harshly. "She was always selfish, but I never imagined… I had to ring your father and let him know what happened. He was distraught. He loved your mother so much. He needed to stay in school. I wanted to get to know my grandchild, and you know the rest."

I gazed at her sympathetically, not knowing what to say. I had never really thought about how bad it must have been for Gran to lose her daughter like that.

"You know, her favourite book growing up was about a little girl called Perdita. She was a sad little character with no real family or friends, always forgotten about. I often thought of it. Every single time you tried to hide away from the limelight." She gestured as if batting away the past. "So. Your mother. I tried to make sure history wouldn't repeat itself. To make sure your father didn't drive you away too, but I suppose I haven't done the best job, have I?"

I knelt beside her and rested my head on her knee. "I won't ever do that, Gran. Any of it. I promise. But I need to find my own way. Even if that's selfish. I can't be who you or Dad want me to be."

She stroked my hair. "I know that, Perdy. We're so caught up in the past that we haven't been paying attention. I swear I'll do better; it's hard to forget things sometimes. You scared us when you said you would leave. We've both been trying our best to let you use your wings. But it'll take time."

We spent the rest of the day together. Closer than we'd been for a long time. I was glad she opened up to me. It made me understand exactly where she and Dad were coming from. She was looking for a second chance, and he was terrified I would make his mistakes. I wasn't planning on letting either of them down.

Chapter Nine

At school the next day, Tammie asked me if I'd go into town with her that evening. I waited for her to turn up for hours, eventually ringing her to see what was going on.

"Oh, sorry," she said. "I'm out with Joey."

"Em, okay. Did you forget you asked me to go to town with you?"

"I went with Joey instead. Listen, I have to go. I'll see you tomorrow, okay?"

She hung up before I could say anything else. I stood there looking at my phone in confusion for a few minutes until it beeped to let me know I had received a text. It was from Amelia asking if I had seen anything nice in town. I texted her back to let her know we hadn't gone. Her next message invited me over. I figured if Dad was going to let me go into town with Tammie, then he wouldn't have a problem with me heading over to Amelia's house, so I agreed.

At Amelia's house, I was half-relieved, half-disappointed to find she was completely alone.

"Where's everyone?"

Her bottom lip jutted out into a sulky pout. "They had to go somewhere and couldn't take me along."

"Oh? Where?" I sort of blurted it out without thinking.

Amelia flushed scarlet. "Um, they're all at the cinema together. Anyway, you're here now. Wanna see my room?"

She led me up the stairs before I could ask her why on earth her family couldn't take her to the pictures with them. I saw even more pictures of wolves.

"Your family really like wolves," I muttered.

She giggled as if I had just made a really funny joke. Her cluttered bedroom was not what I expected. Dream catchers hung around her bed and wind chimes decorated her windows. There were pictures and ornaments all over the place. She was a total hoarder. All of her shelves overflowed.

"Wow," I said, wandering over to her bookshelf. "This is some room." All of her books were on the occult or ancient mythology. I had expected it to be filled with teen romances or something.

"Thanks," she said, beaming. She picked up a small silk bag and pointed at it.

"Want me to do a reading?"

My mind went blank. "A reading?"

"Yeah, like, tarot cards."

"Um, okay. I don't believe in any of that stuff though."

"That's all right. You will soon enough."

I laughed, but she didn't look like she was kidding.

She took a pack of cards from the silk pouch and shuffled them.

"Sit on the bed. I'll do a simple three card reading. One card for your past, your present, and your future."

I gave a careless shrug in reply but sat down and waited. Part of me was intrigued. Part of me thought she might be a little crazy.

"Okay," she said, sitting across from me. "Pick a card, but don't touch it, or I'll have to cleanse them."

"Laying it on a bit thick, aren't we? Okay, that one." I pointed to the middle of the spread deck. She turned the card over, revealing a heart being stabbed by three long swords.

"This is your past. Oh, Perdita, I'm sorry." She bit her lip hard.

"Sorry? Why?"

"The three of swords is a card of sorrow. It says your past was full of conflict, pain, and heartbreak."

"That's just stupid. I don't like this game." An all too familiar lump in my throat horrified me.

"It's not a game! Anyway, it's okay, because the problems lead to a good outcome. Pick another card. One for your present."

I couldn't help rolling my eyes. She had put on a low voice to try and sound mysterious. I pointed to another card. It portrayed a couple holding a pair of cups while a lion's head looked down on them. Amelia practically jumped up and down with glee.

"I knew it! This is the two of cups. It signifies the beginning of a relationship, love, and partnership. And guess what, my brother's single. How lucky!"

"Oh, shut up, and get on with it. That's another rubbish card." I pointed at the final card. The one that would predict my future. One word caught my eye. Death.

"Great," I muttered.

"It's not how it looks. I promise. In fact, it can be a great card. It just means a new beginning. The death is pretty much the end of an old way of life, and the start of something brand new. It foretells major changes in your future. Considering the other two cards, it makes sense, right?"

I couldn't help laughing at the serious look on her face. "Right, Amelia. Makes total sense. I'm sure your pack of cards have my entire life worked out. I told you. I don't believe in this stuff. I don't know why you do."

She glared at me and twisted the charm bracelet on her wrist. "I *believe* because I happen to know there's more to this life than people think. I've seen things most people believe can't be true, so I know for a fact anything's possible." For the first time I caught a glimpse of a fiery little temper.

I raised my hands in protest. "I'm sorry, okay? It's just not for me. I don't believe a card can predict my future. Nobody can. If you want to believe in all this stuff, then go ahead. That's cool for you. Just don't try and do a reading for Tammie, please. If she gets a Death card, she *will* flip out on you."

Amelia laughed along with me, her flash of temper over. I knew I had no right to judge her or the things she believed in, but I still thought her reaction was a little odd.

I left a few hours later. The rest of her family still hadn't returned. No film was *that* long.

Back at home, my Dad was on the warpath.

"Where have you been? I've been trying to ring you for ages. I called Tammie, and she said you hadn't been with her at all. What are you playing at?"

I checked my phone. The battery was dead. "Sorry, I didn't realise my phone was off. Tammie didn't turn up, so I went over to Amelia's house instead. I didn't think you'd mind."

His face was pink with anger. I had no idea what his problem was. "You know quite well you need to let me know where you are. I brought Erin back here to have dinner with us, but you weren't here, and you couldn't be bothered to even switch your phone on."

I got annoyed too. "I didn't know the phone was off! For God's sake, stop overreacting! I was twenty minutes away for a couple of hours. How was I supposed to know you'd want me to be here for dinner? Get a grip!" I stormed out of the room and went upstairs, ignoring him when he ordered me back.

The next morning, Tammie sent me a text saying she was getting a lift to school with Joey. I wasn't invited. Gran noticed how glum I was over breakfast.

"Something wrong?"

I shrugged. "Not much. It's just, I feel weird today. Tammie's going to school with Joey this morning, and she pretty much made it clear I'm not welcome." I decided not to tell her about the row I had with Dad.

"Hmm, well, you did say they were getting closer. Maybe you should give her a chance to figure out where they're headed. She's always having to fight for attention at home. Maybe she needs one on one time for a change."

"Suppose." I still felt left out and wasn't looking forward to getting the bus alone.

I huddled into the corner of my seat on the bus, feeling lonelier than ever. Now that my life was opening up in some ways, other parts of it were slipping away. If I was honest, I resented the way Tammie was ditching me in her attempt to "make progress" with Joey. Who does that? Ditches their friend for a boy? It made me wonder if she had only ever been my friend to get close to him.

I was so engrossed in my thoughts that I didn't even notice Nathan and Amelia sit down until Nathan nudged me.

"Are you okay?" he asked.

"Yeah, sorry, I'm fine. Just in a world of my own here." I sat up straight and tried to focus.

"Where's Tammie?" Amelia said as she rummaged through her school bag for something.

"She got a lift with Joey this morning."

She stopped what she was doing to stare at me. "Is that how it sounds?"

I shrugged. "I don't mind."

Amelia frowned and stared at me, waiting for me to say more.

"Really, I don't care."

"Well, I wouldn't like it," she decided.

"Her loss," Nathan said.

I wanted them to leave it alone, so I did my best to change the subject.

"So. How are my doggy mates today?"

"Pining for you," Nathan teased.

"I'll bet. They've experienced the greatness of me, and now they're stuck with you. It must be so terribly disappointing for them."

"Cheeky."

I grinned at him, but then something seemed to catch in my throat. I lost myself in his eyes, and all I could think about was what it would be like to kiss him right there and then.

"Perdita?" he said quizzically.

"Sorry, spaced out there," I said, shaking my head in confusion. The last thing on my mind had been how much I liked him, yet there I was getting all gooey eyed in front of him. I had to get my act together before I made a complete fool of myself. The weekend before had made me too used to his company.

Both Amelia and Nathan seemed much more relaxed without Tammie around. I had always known Tammie could be brash, but I didn't realise they were uncomfortable around her because of it.

That morning I didn't share a class with Tammie, so Nathan sat next to me.

"Did you enjoy yourself at the weekend?" I asked him. "I kept Amelia company," I added, when I saw him look confused.

"Oh. Right. Yep, we drove up North to visit some old friends of the family." He fidgeted and looked away, but I already knew he was lying. And Amelia too, probably. Weird.

I saw Tammie between classes, but she breezed past me without even saying hello. I followed her, laughing, thinking she was joking, but she kept on walking. I pulled her arm to stop her.

"Hey, what's the matter with you? Blind today? You just walked straight past me."

She sighed and turned around, like it was some great effort. The way she looked at me sent a shiver down my spine. Had I done something? Panic set in. The way it always had when we were young. If she wanted me to do something I didn't want to do, she'd give me that look. As if she was going to withhold her friendship or something. And I'd be so scared of not having a friend that I'd do whatever she wanted.

"What's wrong?" I asked, my voice quivering.

"Nothing." She looked bored.

"Seriously, what's up with you?"

Her eyes narrowed. "Apart from you wrecking my head, you mean?"

"What did I do?" She rolled her eyes at my words, and I began to feel annoyed. I hadn't done anything wrong. "Tammie, I asked you a question. I don't know what you have to be angry about. *I* should be the angry one after you left me waiting yesterday."

"Oh, get over it. It's no big deal, for God's sake."

"It *is* a big deal. I went over to Amelia's in the end, and my Dad flipped 'cos you told him you hadn't seen me at all."

"Eh, don't blame me because you can't do what you're told, Perdy."

"Are you for real?" I couldn't believe what she was saying.

"You're such a child sometimes. Throwing your toys out of the pram because we didn't invite you," she sneered.

"But you *did* invite me!"

"So I changed my mind. Is that so bad?"

"No. Not really," I said, subdued. Maybe I was over-reacting.

"Well, then."

"All right, I'm sorry. But why didn't you get the bus with me? Or even ask me to get a lift with you?"

"Christ, you're really doing my head in. Do you invite me when you go to Amelia's house? Do I moan at you when you spend all your time giggling with *her*?" Tammie's eyes glittered with anger.

"No, but…"

"See?" she said, sounding triumphant.

"But that's different! I can't invite you to someone else's house!"

"And I can't invite you to get a lift in someone else's car, so stop whining Perdy." She looked so exasperated that I took a step backward. I couldn't understand why she was no angry with me. Amelia ran over to us, completely oblivious to what was happening.

"Oh, great. It's your new buddy." Tammie rolled her eyes.

Amelia and I exchanged baffled looks.

"Look, Perdy," Tammie continued. "I get that you're jealous. And I know you're totally spoiled and think everything should be all about you, all of the time. But you have to understand the world does not revolve around you, alright?"

"What's going on?" Amelia asked. I struggled to find words.

"Perdy's going mad because Joey and I want to spend time together." Tammie looked so smug that she reminded me of Dawn.

"I'm not!" I protested. "You're the one who blanked me before. I don't know why you're so annoyed with me."

"Whatever." Tammie walked away.

"Tammie, wait!" I called after her. She ignored me. Tears slid down my cheeks. Tammie had been my friend forever, and suddenly she was acting as if she didn't care about me. I didn't even know why. I still couldn't see why she was angry with me; it made me sick to the pit of my stomach.

"What a cow." Amelia shook her head in disgust.

"I don't get it," I said, struggling to figure out what had just happened.

"She's just a cow. Come on. Let's go," she said, tugging on my arm.

I shrugged her off. "Don't say that. She's my friend, all right?"

Amelia's eyes widened in surprise. "But Perdita, she just spoke to you like crap. You don't need that. Why would you want to be her friend?"

Tears fell again—this time frustrated, angry tears. "Why don't you just mind your own business?" I snapped. "Keep out of it."

She looked so hurt that I was instantly contrite. "I'm sorry, I didn't mean…"

"Oh, forget it," she said and walked away in a huff.

I spent the entire day alone. It seemed as though the whole world was mad at me. Nathan glared coldly at me as he sympathised with his sister later that morning. Tammie sat next to Joey in every class. All day, I felt sick and unwelcome.

At lunch, Joey and Tammie were already at our table. They both stood and left as soon as I sat down. My stomach churned again. All I wanted to do was cry. Joey hadn't even looked at me. I still had no idea why Tammie was mad at me, never mind Joey.

I spotted Nathan and Amelia walk into the lunch room together, deep in conversation. I knew I was the one to blame. I turned on Amelia because I was upset with Tammie and cost myself a friend. I decided I couldn't face yet another cold shoulder, so I snuck outside and spent my lunch break feeling miserable.

At home, Dad was still angry with me. He banged doors and pointedly ignored me, leaving me shivering inside. I tried ringing Tammie, but she didn't answer. I rang Amelia that evening, prepared to grovel.

"Please don't hang up on me, Amelia. I know you're mad at me, and I deserve it. I just want you to know that I'm sorry. I swear, I didn't mean it."

"It's okay. I know."

"You're not mad?"

"Of course not. I looked for you at lunch, but you weren't around. I could *never* stay angry with you."

She sounded oddly adamant, but I was just relieved I still had a friend somewhere. We talked about what had happened with Tammie that morning.

"Look," Amelia said, after I filled her in on everything. "She was probably in a bad mood and took it out on you. I think she was bang out of order, but I'm going to keep out of it because I know you really like her. So tomorrow, we go speak to her and get it sorted. She'll have calmed down by then. She's probably feeling just as bad as you."

Tammie didn't get the bus the next morning. For the second time in a row, Nathan sat beside me for the entire journey. I felt better with him next to me.

Tammie sat with Joey in our first class. I stayed in my usual seat and pretty much sulked. Everything was changing. It was as if I had been asleep for a few weeks, and now I was struggling to catch up. Tammie was effectively freezing me out for no reason other than to spend more time with my cousin.

I tried to apologise to her between classes. Her friendship meant more to me than my pride. Or at least, I thought it did. We had been friends for years. That had to be worth something, right? I wanted to be a good friend, but the more I thought about it, the more sure I was that Tammie was the one in the wrong. Still, I missed the familiarity—we had been through a lot together. Maybe that was enough to overlook how she was acting. Despite trying to talk me out of it, Amelia joined me for moral support.

"Look Tammie, I know we had a row, but can't we forget about it now? We're best friends. It's silly to avoid each other over nothing. I'm sorry I brought up you going out with Joey instead of me."

I regretted it the instant I saw how disgusted she looked.

"Aw, I don't care, Perdy. Would you ever get some dignity or something?"

"What?"

"Stop crawling after me. I'm not interested. Get it now? Joey and me, we don't need you tagging along anymore. Stick to your new little friends, all right?" She glared at Amelia.

"What the hell is your problem?" I said, too astonished to respond in any other way.

"Back *off*, I said." She shoved me, forcing me backward. Too stunned to react, I gaped at Tammie, waiting for her to laugh. She didn't.

Amelia stepped toward Tammie, but I couldn't hear what she said. I was too busy freaking out inside my head. I didn't recognise Tammie anymore. She looked Amelia up and down then stormed off.

"Are you okay?" Amelia said.

I nodded, still stunned. "Did that just happen?"

"Oh, yeah. It definitely happened. Told you she's a cow."

I spent the rest of the day trying to figure out what was going on. I couldn't think of anything that would make my best friend suddenly hate me.

Nathan joined me at lunch. It was nice to have someone to talk to when Tammie and Joey sat down and ignored me. They instantly huddled together as though they had lots of secrets to share. Paranoia weaved itself around me. I was sure they were whispering about me.

"Cheer up." Nathan nudged me.

"Consider me cheered," I said, but I felt comforted by his presence.

Things took a turn for the worse when Dawn decided to sidle over to the table.

"Oh, my God, Nathan. You have to walk me home today."

"I do? Why's that now?" His tone was even, but he looked like he was hanging on to his last thread of patience.

"Didn't you hear? I got attacked last night!" For an instant, the fear in her voice sounded genuine.

"Attacked? Really?" I could tell Nathan already disbelieved whatever story she was going to come up with.

She nodded. "This gigantic dog came after me last night, snarling at me with these *huge* teeth. It was terrifying, I swear. It ran straight at me then at the last second it, like, skidded to a stop and ran off."

"Maybe it caught your stench." Tammie smiled sweetly at Dawn who scowled at her then turned back to Nathan.

"You know I don't like dogs, and you're used to them, so maybe you could come with me, please? It was like a wolf, for real."

Nathan's whole body tensed up, but Amelia turned up before Dawn could get an answer from him. Dawn didn't wait; she told him she would see him later. Amelia took over the conversation, so I didn't have to think. Or talk for that matter. I was in a daydream when Aaron sat down beside me. He touched my back lightly, giving me what he thought was a charming smile. I edged away; I didn't like him, and I didn't want his hands anywhere near me.

"So, ladies," he said, looking at me and Amelia. "You're both coming to my party on Saturday night, right?"

Amelia and I exchanged horrified looks. I couldn't think of anything less fun. "Um, I don't think…"

"Yeah, of course we'll come," Tammie butted in.

Aaron frowned. He hadn't actually invited her or Joey. "Oh, okay. I'll see you all there then?"

Tammie snorted with laughter. "As if. No way would Perdy be allowed go. She's not even allowed stay over in my house."

"Maybe her Dad just doesn't like *you*, Tammie," Amelia said coolly.

Tammie glared at Amelia for a few seconds before turning back to Aaron. "Like I said, *we'll* be there. No point even asking her."

Aaron looked completely confused by the proceedings. He gave a watery smile and left in a hurry. Actually, I was completely confused too. Tammie sounded hateful when she spoke about me. As though it was my fault my Dad was strict. As though she had a right to even bring it up in conversation when somebody invited me somewhere. She purposely tried to make me seem silly and childish.

Whatever was up with Tammie and Joey, they had made me determined to go to the party. Normally, I wouldn't have been the slightest bit interested, but seeing as she had pretty much called me out, I felt as though I had to go. The only problem was Dad.

We had a rare family dinner that evening. Dad seemed like he was in a good humour, so I decided to broach the subject.

"Dad," I said, hoping I had a face a father couldn't refuse. "I was just wondering… you see, there's this party."

"No," he said firmly, not bothering to look up from his food.

"You didn't even let me finish," I said, annoyed at his resistance.

"You're not going to any party."

"But *Dad...*" Even I could hear the whine in my voice.

"Stephen, at least hear her out."

Dad glared at my grandmother. My stomach ached. I sensed trouble brewing between them again. I hated when things were like this, but I had to go to that party.

"Fine, Dad, give me one good reason why not." I knew he wouldn't have one. At least one that was good enough for me.

He dropped his fork onto his plate with a clang. "You mean apart from your recent behaviour? Okay, I don't want you at parties. I don't want you anywhere unsupervised. I don't want you near boys or any possibility of alcohol, drugs, or anything else. I want to keep you safe."

"By keeping me locked away? You're supposed to be smart, but you can't see how stupid your rules are. I'm going to move away to college as soon as I leave school. How am I supposed to know how to look after myself? How will I know how to deal with different situations or peer pressure or anything when you won't let me have any kind of experiences now? You're going to wait until everything is legal, and then let me go wild. Is that it?" My voice was now shrill.

"Don't scream at me. Go to your room." He picked up his fork and went back to his dinner as if he didn't even care how I felt.

"With bloody pleasure," I shouted, before stomping up the stairs and slamming my bedroom door behind me. Okay, maybe having a bit of a teenage meltdown wasn't a good way to handle things, but quiet obedience obviously wasn't doing anything for me either.

I stayed in my room that evening, moaning to Amelia about my Dad through instant messaging, but I really wanted to talk to Tammie. I missed her. Even though she had been horrible to me.

I left the house the next morning without speaking a word to my father. I could tell he was angry, but I did not care.

At school, Joey confronted me as though I was in the wrong.

"Perdy, what's going on with you and Tammie? Why did you pick a fight with her?"

"What are you on about, Joe?" I was seriously baffled.

"You won't sit with her, talk to her, or anything. You're bitching about us behind our backs. What's happening to you? She told me how you ditched her the other night and practically attacked her yesterday. What's wrong with you, Perdy? Ever since Amelia and Nathan came along, things have been different. It's not fair to ditch your old friends just 'cos some new ones come along."

"Are you bloody well crazy? Or do you just believe everything that's whispered into your ear?" I saw black spots in front of my eyes, I was so angry. "Next time somebody says I did something, maybe you should make sure it's true before accusing me of things!"

I stalked off in a temper. The males in my family were really getting on my nerves.

***

At lunch the next day, all five of us sat around the table in awkward, tense silence. Joey had been looking thoughtful for about ten minutes, the kind of look that guaranteed he was chewing something over in his mind. When he spoke, we all paid attention.

"Tammie, when did Perdy stop sitting next to you in class and on the bus?"

All of our heads shot up as one. Amelia almost spat out her drink in her hurry to speak before Tammie, whose face drained of colour.

"What are you talking about, Joey? Perdy always sits beside Tammie on the bus. Except when Tammie gets lifts with you," Amelia said, quick as a flash.

"And she hasn't moved from her usual seat in any class I've been in," Nathan added. "But Tammie sits with you now, right?"

Neither of them had lied or accused Tammie of anything, but she looked at them with pure hatred in her eyes.

"I see," Joey said, his brain ticking over. "And what was the argument about? When Perdy shoved Tammie away?"

Amelia snorted derisively, but I was too stunned to speak. "You've got it the wrong way around there, Joey. And in case you've been misinformed, Perdy tried to sort things out, but Tammie was too busy telling her not to tag along with you two anymore to listen."

I felt ill, but as soon as Nathan held my hand under the table, my head cleared, and I could think straight. It was slowly dawning on me what was really happening. My best friend had stabbed me in the back and tried to turn my cousin against me. But why?

"So, Tammie, you lied to me?" Joey's voice stayed at the same volume, but it had gone icy cold. I shivered myself at the look he was giving her, more than glad it wasn't directed at me.

She opened her mouth and stuttered something. It was clear she assumed Joey would never bring it up in front of us all. He wasn't one for big confrontations. Joey didn't give her another chance to make an excuse.

"I take it everything else you've been saying to me is complete bull then, yeah?"

Her guilty expression told him everything he needed to know, as far as he was concerned. I saw that change in his face. He turned to me.

"Perdy, I'm sorry I didn't check with you first. I hope you can forgive me."

"Of course," I said. I had been mad at him, but he was family. That was more important than anything else.

Joey stood up slowly, nodded and walked away from us. Tammie didn't wait, rushing after him to try and repair things.

"Wow," Nathan said, releasing my hand. "That was awkward."

"I wonder what else she's been telling him," Amelia said, but she looked kind of delighted.

"You okay?" Nathan turned to look at me.

"Why would she lie about me? She's been my only friend forever. I don't get it." I couldn't figure it out.

Amelia was hesitant for a second. Perhaps unsure if I really wanted an answer. "Don't you ever think she's a bit of an attention seeker? Maybe she did it so Joey would feel sorry for her or something."

I tried to grasp that idea. "Lying about me to get Joey's attention? Would that even work?"

I looked to Nathan for an answer. He squirmed in his seat. "It kinda did work, Perdita. He believed her and went along with it. After all, why would someone lie about that? If he wasn't your cousin, he might never have thought of getting it all out in the open."

I felt a little sick. Did I really mean that little to her?

"Did you ask your Dad about the party?" Amelia tried to change the subject.

I made a face. "Yeah. Actually, he didn't let me ask. I said the word party, and he shut down. No, as always."

"I'm sure he'll change his mind," she said, unconcerned.

"Hasn't happened yet." I was getting grumpier by the second.

Tammie didn't turn up to the next class. I found her afterwards in the bathroom, still crying. For once, she didn't care who saw how red her eyes were. She grabbed me, almost hysterical in her urgency. It freaked me out a little.

"You have to talk to him, Perdy. You have to. He hates me now!"

I shrugged. "That's your fault. Why should I help you?"

"Please, I'm begging here. I know it was stupid, but I thought it would be okay for a few days, that he'd spend more time with me then ask me out or something. I didn't think you'd even notice. You've been stuck to Amelia lately. I was desperate. I didn't know what else to do! Besides, you told me I had to do something, and come on, even you have to admit you've been all over the new kids any chance you've gotten."

I couldn't believe she was trying to turn the blame on me. "I didn't tell you to screw me over, Tams! How could you do that to me?"

"I didn't mean to cause any problems." She saw my face and changed her tone. "Okay, maybe a little part of me wanted to punish you. You're acting like you don't need me anymore, and it bugs me. I've been feeling a little… jealous of you and Amelia, and it all got out of hand. I just wanted him to notice me. That's all." She wiped away fresh tears.

I looked her over and decided I believed her. Sort of. I noted she hadn't said sorry. Part of me understood what she was trying to do. As stupid as I thought it was. More importantly, I realised I didn't know her as well as I had always thought—she didn't value our friendship at all. I'd watched her 'punish' people for years. I just didn't think I would end up getting the same treatment.

"Okay, I'll talk to him." I agreed. Partly to get away from her, and partly because I wanted everything out in the open. My cousin deserved to know the whole truth in order to make a decision.

In our last class, I sat next to him. He wouldn't talk to me about Tammie but eventually agreed to show up at my house after school.

Gran was still around when I got home.

"Gran, could you give me a few minutes with Joey when he comes over?"

"Why? What's going on?"

"Nothing much. Just some drama between Joey and Tammie. She asked me to put in a good word for her."

Gran frowned, her wrinkles creasing. "It's never a good idea to interfere, Perdy. Especially when it's between two people you're close to. If it all goes wrong, you'll be the one picking up the pieces."

"It'll be fine, Gran. I know what I'm doing."

She didn't look convinced, but I couldn't see how it could go wrong.

Joey looked tired when he arrived. Quiet in a defeated way. I wasn't sure if he would listen because he stuck out his chin stubbornly when I mentioned Tammie's name.

"She's really upset because you won't talk to her."

"Why do you care? I mean, she lied about you. That's messed up. What kind of a friend does that? We're family."

"Ah, Joey, I know she's done wrong, but she's… she's desperate." I wasn't sure how to convince him when I wasn't convinced.

"For what? Did she enjoy messing with my head too much? Is she sad it's all over? Because I don't want to talk to her again. I don't like being lied to. You know that." His hands shook, and I could tell he was taking it personally.

"How about I tell you some truths then?" I said, hoping to make him feel better. "She's been mad about you for years, and you've never looked at her twice. Everybody knows she likes you, maybe you do too, and you just don't care. But, whatever. It's probably all my fault she lied to you anyway."

He almost went cross eyed with confusion. "What? What does that mean? What do you mean mad about me? And how does that end up with you being at fault anyhow?"

"Oh, come on, Joey. It's only obvious. I mean, she flirts with you all the time. She does everything she can to make you notice her and still no joy. Then I sort of said something to her." I faltered, reluctant to take the blame.

Looking bewildered, he tried to grasp what I was telling him. I could almost see him looking at memories through different eyes. After a few minutes his face cleared.

"What did you say to her?"

"Erm, I sort of told her she should tell you before anyone else took a fancy to you. I was just trying to give her a kick up the arse with it. I didn't know she'd go cuckoo and make up a story for a pity party. When I told her to get your attention, I meant by coming clean about how she feels, not by trying to get you to feel sorry for her or anything."

He scratched his head. It was almost funny to watch someone so smart feel so stupid. Slowly, ever so slowly, a smile crept across his face. I laughed, relieved.

"So, this is good news?"

"I can't say it makes me feel bad. She's liked me all this time? How did I not see that?" He rubbed his forehead as if he was trying to help the news to sink in.

"I really don't know. You don't have much common sense sometimes. So what's the story? Do you like her, too?" I crossed my fingers out of habit.

"I don't know. I mean, she's pretty, but I've never really thought about things that way before. I... it wouldn't be horrible to go out with her, I suppose."

"I'm sure that would be good enough for a start." I ignored how unenthusiastic he sounded.

"But still, that was a pretty devious thing she did. She tried to make me think bad of you. That's bang out of order."

"Yeah, I know. I'm not saying she should get away with anything, but everyone deserves a second chance, and in fairness, she's not likely to do it again. Put it down to a moment of madness or something."

He thought about it. "You're very forgiving."

"I'm not really. I just don't know how I would have acted if I was in her shoes."

He raised his eyebrows. "I highly doubt you would tell Nathan that Amelia was being a bitch to you just to get his attention."

"Oh, you notice when *I* like someone," I blurted.

"So, it's true then."

I figured my blush was enough of an answer to that one.

"Just be careful," he warned.

"Nothing's going to happen there. Don't worry."

"Hmm, we'll see. There's something about him that's a bit... off, just watch yourself."

"Not you as well," I said, exasperated. "If you got that from Tammie, then don't forget she doesn't exactly have the best judgement right now."

He shrugged. "Well, thanks for telling me all this. 'Bout time someone did. Anything I can do for you?"

"Unless you can give my Dad a complete personality transplant, then no."

He smiled. "Take it the party idea didn't go down well."

"Yup. Big surprise there."

"So, what are you going to do?"

"What can I do? Wait until I can move out, and then go crazy is all." My new motto.

"Not the greatest plan, Perdy."

I rolled my eyes. The problem with Joey was he usually came with a big dose of sensible.

"What if I talked to him?" It was a nice offer, but I doubted Dad would suddenly listen to Joey. He seemed to think it was worth a try. He waited until my Dad came home to give it a shot.

"I'll be around at about eight on Saturday to pick up Perdy," he told my Dad.

"Pick her up for what?"

"The party, of course."

My Dad burst out laughing. "Nice try. No chance."

"What time does she have to be back at?" Joey didn't give in easily.

This time Dad gave him a pitying look.

"All right," Joey said. "I'll tutor her in French for a month if she goes."

Interesting. Joey had upped the stakes dramatically. French was my weak point, and Dad always despaired of my poor results in tests, somehow convinced that failing French would ruin my life for all eternity. He ignored me whenever I reminded him I planned on applying to the College of Art and Design. French wasn't exactly a requirement.

For the first time ever, my Dad considered backing down. It was amazing. Joey, my hero.

"Okay," Dad said, still thinking hard. "If you tutor her for a month, then she can go to the party. But she has to be home by ten."

"Midnight."

I was beginning to feel like Cinderella.

"Eleven." The pain of conceding an hour showed on Dad's face.

"Midnight, and I'll throw in an extra weekend of French." Joey grinned, confident Dad would weaken.

I could see Dad desperately wanted to say no, but his head wouldn't let him. Six weeks of one on one time with Joey's brain was too valuable to pass up. Finally, he nodded his agreement. I gave a little yelp of excitement and hugged Joey as hard as I could.

"I owe you big time," I said as soon as Dad left the room, trying not to squeal.

"Too right you do. Anyway, I better head off. Do me a favour. Tell Tammie not to bother me for a few days, okay? I need space."

"Of course," I said, but I wondered if they would ever be okay again. Everything had changed.

Once he left, I rang Amelia to tell her what happened. She was predictably excited.

Afterwards, I hesitated when it came to telling Tammie. Things didn't feel the same anymore. She let me down, and I wasn't sure if I trusted her. I promised Joey I'd pass on his message, so I took a deep breath and rang her. She sounded subdued when she answered the phone.

"Tams, it's me. Listen, I spoke to Joey."

"What did he say?"

"He needs a bit of time away from you. He's still pissed, but I explained things so maybe—"

"How much time?" she blurted out, interrupting me.

"Uh, a few days. He'll be at the party, so he'll probably chat to you there."

She seemed okay with that, but she got off the phone as quickly as possible. There was a distance between us that I didn't think could ever be bridged. More importantly, I was going to the party. Nathan would be there too. Things were looking up.

Chapter Ten

Thoughts of the party kept me awake at night. First proper house party. Nathan would be there. Something could happen. Maybe. Or I could make a fool of myself. Likely. At least Amelia would be there. Joey and Tammie would probably sort things out, and I could keep on ignoring the fact he wasn't as interested in her as she was in him.

School was quiet. Tammie and I were still tense and awkward around each other, Joey avoided us all, and Amelia had a sore throat.

"Are you going to be up for the party?" I asked Amelia anxiously as she sneezed for the fourth time in a row.

"Sure," she said, after blowing her nose. "I'll be fine by then."

By Friday, she could barely speak. I kept my distance at the bus stop after school in case she sneezed on me again. Nathan soon joined us, accompanied by Aaron and Abbi.

"So are you still going to my party?" Aaron asked me.

"I think so."

"Is your Dad letting you go?" Abbi said, her voice full of surprise.

"Yes." I was a little snappier than I should have been.

"Cool," Aaron said, beaming. "How about you, Amelia?"

"As long as this cold doesn't get worse," she croaked.

"Don't forget to bring your own drinks," he reminded us.

"Should be fun," Abbi said, smiling at me—I couldn't bring myself to share her enthusiasm.

"Can I talk to you for a sec?" Nathan whispered to me. We walked away from the others, and excitement brewed inside me as I wondered what he might say to me.

He shoved his hands in his pockets and avoided my eyes. "Look, I know you and Abbi haven't been friends in the past, but give her a chance, okay? She's cool."

"Um, what?" Seriously?

"I saw how you looked at her just there. She's trying to be nice to you. I just thought... I'd say something." He flushed red and walked away. I watched him as he joined the others, wondering if it was Abbi he was interested in. Not even the now familiar sight of a man with red hair watching us from across the street could distract me from that thought.

***

Saturday brought a whole new set of problems. Important ones, like what to wear. I changed outfits numerous times until Gran finally stepped in to help. Girlifying me was right up her street.

At eight on the dot, Joey and Tammie arrived. Dad looked so grumpy that I said goodbye before he changed his mind.

"Have a wonderful evening." Gran hugged me close to her. "You look just like your mother," she whispered in my ear. Maybe that wasn't helping Dad's mood.

It was a little awkward for a while with Joey and Tammie. They still hadn't sorted things out. Joey kept glancing at Tammie's legs, so I figured that was a good sign.

Aaron stood in his garden with some of his friends when we arrived. He waved and told us to go on in and get comfortable. It was still early, not many people had shown up yet, so we were able to grab a seat.

I saw Nathan in the living room and waved him over, looking for Amelia.

"Didn't she tell you? Our grandmother is making her stay in bed all weekend."

"Aw, no." I didn't simply mean because Amelia was still sick. I was also dreading the thoughts of being at the party without her. "Should I bring her something?"

He shook his head, smiling. "She'll be fine. She's being spoiled as we speak." He touched my arm lightly. "I'm glad you came, Perdita. You look nice."

My cheeks instantly heated up. Dawn called him over before I could reply. He rolled his eyes.

"I better go see what she wants before she comes over here and wrecks your head. See you in a bit."

He headed over to Dawn who pulled him close beside her. I tried to ignore the jealous twinges in my gut.

I was soon bored stiff. The house was filling up, but I sat on the arm of a chair occupied by Tammie and Joey who whispered intently together. Third wheel alert. When Tammie stood up and announced she was going to speak with Joey in private, I couldn't help groaning. She ignored me and dragged him upstairs. I watched her go; half-hoping she could sense the hate vibes I sent her way.

For a while, I waited for them, sipping a can of coke, watching people dance, and listening to a group of boys exaggerate about a gang of feral dogs running around our estate. I was more interested in the dancing. Nathan and Abbi danced together quite a lot but within a group of people. When Dawn wasn't throwing me daggers, I was able to watch them unnoticed. People flocked around Nathan while Aaron watched from across the room, scowling whenever his gaze fell upon Nathan.

Watching everyone have a good time together made me ache inside. I wanted to go home. Parties were no fun for people like me. I felt too awkward and out of place. Too afraid of making a fool of myself.

"You going to dance or what?" Nathan asked when he stopped to get a drink, his cheeks pink with heat from dancing. I glanced over at Dawn. Her sneer made me shrink back into myself.

"Uh, no. Maybe later."

I kept checking the stairs to see if Joey and Tammie were coming back. Waiting around for them on my own was mortifying. I must have looked like such a loner.

By ten o'clock, I decided enough was enough. I was going home. I headed outside, passed by a gang of slightly drunk boys unnoticed, and began the walk home.

I passed by the woods and heard a noise that stopped me in my tracks. A low growl behind me. Looking around, I saw nothing on the path. Shivering a little, I kept walking, but a sudden flash of movement to my right had me whirling around in fright. Breathing heavily, I reminded myself it was just an animal. Probably a hungry stray dog. I took a deep breath and kneeled down, steeling myself. Peering through the trees, I strained my eyes looking for whatever had growled. If it was the stray dog that killed the cat outside my door, then maybe I could feed it so it wouldn't need to kill anything else.

"Here doggy," I called.

"What are you doing, Perdita?"

I jumped to my feet with fright. "Oh. Nothing."

Nathan approached me with a bemused smile on his face.

Blushing, I gestured toward the woods. "I thought I heard a growl. I was trying to get the dog to come out."

He looked in the direction I was pointing. I could have sworn I saw him sniff the air. "There's nothing there."

"There was. I swear."

"I believe you, but it's gone now." He said it with a smile that didn't reach his eyes. "You're positive you heard a growl?"

"Oh, yeah. There's a stray running around, I think. After we bumped into you in the cinema that night? I kept thinking I heard a dog all the way home."

He looked startled. "Did you see it?"

"Not right then, but the next morning there was a dead cat on my doorstep, so Dad reckoned it was a stray dog. Oh, wait, I saw a dog outside my house later that night. Remember I told you? It was bigger than Cúchulainn. Sort of looked like a wolf." I laughed, half-joking.

He froze, a flicker of fear crossing his face when I wanted him to tell me I was being silly, and it was just a dog. Then another thought occurred to me.

"Wait, what are *you* doing here?"

He blushed. "Oh, well, I saw you leave, and I thought I'd see if you were coming back or what. But Dawn got in the way so you were already gone. I didn't catch up until now."

I looked away; I didn't want to think about the party. "I didn't think Tammie and Joey were going to come back, so there was no point staying."

"Come back with me for a little while."

I shook my head. "It's not my thing. I was really bored."

"That's because you didn't dance!"

"People think I'm bad enough without me dancing by myself, Nathan." I squirmed at the idea of him knowing what people thought of me. Wondered if maybe he was nice to me out of pity.

"You wouldn't have been by yourself though. There were lots of people dancing." I shouldn't have expected him to understand.

"Your friends don't like me, Nathan. You know that. I don't fit in with them," I said, hoping he would leave it.

"Well, come back and have one dance with just me, and then I'll walk you home."

I tried not to look too pleased with the idea. "I don't need to be chaperoned home you know."

"Yeah, well, don't want you getting bitten by any stray dogs. Come on. Just one dance. Please?"

He smiled in that charming way of his that made my insides melt. I couldn't help thinking, *why am I arguing?* Without Dawn's disapproving stare, saying yes to him was a lot easier. Besides, I didn't want to go home early to my Dad's smug face.

Back at the party, Aaron made a show of pulling me toward him, leering the whole time. I wrinkled my nose at the stench of stale beer.

"Come over here with me," he said, so loud I froze, unsure of myself.

Nathan put his hand behind my back and led me away. "Maybe later, Aaron. She owes me a dance first."

Aaron's friends laughed and jeered. I could almost feel Nathan vibrating with annoyance beside me. He laid my jacket across the back of a chair, took my hand and led me into the middle of the room that had been emptied to make a mini dance floor. He clasped my fingers tight, as if expecting me to run. Maybe I would have, but I enjoyed the look of disgust on Dawn's face first. Abbi winked at me, making me think that maybe she wasn't so bad after all.

Nathan guided me to a relatively empty space. The music changed to something a lot slower. People paired off around us. "Oh," I said, backing away. "I should sit down."

"You promised me a dance. Come on. It's just a dance."

I nodded, but I didn't move. Nathan rubbed his jaw. "You're really going to make this hard for me, aren't you?"

He stepped toward me, his eyes so full of amusement that I had to look away. Clearing his throat, he took one of my hands and put it on his shoulder, then dropped his hand to my waist. Every touch felt as though it left a trail of sparks on my skin.

He touched my other hand, brought it close to his heart, and held it there. I could feel his heartbeat drum against my fingertips. He called my name softly. I couldn't look at him without blushing, and

I couldn't look at everyone else without chickening out, so I stared at my hand on his shoulder instead.

He held me closer and sang along to the song under his breath. Said my name again. I chanced looking up at him and regretted it straight away. Being so close to him was a mistake; I would never get over him if I kept letting myself get sucked back in.

"Are you okay?" he asked. I nodded, but his expression stopped me from speaking. He never took his eyes off me, and I forgot all about everyone else. I let myself soak up his gaze, the fire on my skin wherever he touched me, the almost unbearable fluttering inside, the longing in his eyes that matched my own.

He gripped my hand tight. I don't think he realised how hard he was squeezing until I winced. He apologised and let go, only to gently brush his thumb across my cheek. Such a simple thing, and yet it caused my whole body to shudder.

I wished he would kiss me.

He slipped both arms around me, and this time I moved closer, relishing how it felt to lean against his chest, but the song ended, and we pulled apart slowly, reluctantly.

"I wish it was always like this with us," I blurted. His eyes widened with alarm, and he took a step backward. A step away from me—again.

It hit me then how close we had been. I couldn't stand the look in his eyes without trembling. It was too much, only for him to blow cold again. I struggled to catch my breath. The sudden realization that the whole room was focused solely on us unleashed the wave of panic that had been building up within all evening.

"I need to go now," I said. "I don't need you to walk with me. I just have to get out of here."

He nodded and followed me anyway. So many pairs of eyes were on us; my first instinct had always been to run. All of a sudden everything Nathan said or did seemed like something private and intimate, but it was all one-sided because he didn't feel the same way. I pushed blindly past everyone, avoiding their eyes, desperate to get outside.

I made it to the door, but Joey got in my way.

"Where are you going?" He held out his hands to stop me.

"Home."

"Well, wait a second. We'll walk with you," he said. Tammie made an impatient noise beside him.

"It's fine. Stay. I have to go," I said.

"I'm not letting you go alone," Joey said. "If you get attacked by that imaginary wild dog everyone's going hysterical over, your Dad will kill me."

"Oh, just leave her Joey." Tammie sounded impatient, but he frowned at her.

"I'll take her home," Nathan volunteered.

Joey glanced at me. "I don't think that's the best idea."

While they were arguing, Abbi ran over to me and surprised me with a quick hug.

"I'm so glad you came," she gushed.

"Erm, okay, thanks."

"No, really. I used to think you were really stuck up, but you're just shy, right? Anyway, Nathan was *so* happy you turned up, 'cos everyone told him you wouldn't."

She gave me another hug before wandering off to embrace some other random person. I turned my attention back to Nathan who was telling Joey and Tammie to stay and enjoy themselves and that he would probably be back in a while. Tammie whispered something into Joey's ear making him more agreeable to it.

"We'll see you tomorrow," Tammie said, but I was already walking away.

I needed fresh air. Lots of it. Outside, Aaron made a grab at me. This time he pulled me close to him and didn't let go. I could smell rubbish body spray and rancid sweat all over him. I tried to back away, but he held tight, a stupid drunken grin on his face. Some of his friends cheered.

"Leave it out." Gavin, one of the football players, tried his best to calm things down.

I pushed at Aaron until he let go of my arm. I tried to get away, but I walked straight into Nathan. His jaw twitched with anger, and his pupils were dilating rapidly; I couldn't stop staring. Nobody else seemed to notice but, to me, he looked dangerous.

"What are you playing at?" he said to Aaron who laughed.

"It's later, man."

"Leave her alone." He spoke through clenched teeth.

Nathan pushed me behind him as Aaron lurched toward us. He squared up to Nathan who didn't flinch. That infuriated Aaron. He pushed hard, but Nathan didn't budge. Aaron must have been drunker than I thought. Gavin pulled Aaron backward, just in time because he was about to throw a punch. Things were getting out of hand for no apparent reason. Whatever bothered Aaron about Nathan was boiling over because he was drunk and stupid. Reacting to it was even worse. I wasn't interested in seeing it. Especially when I felt so rejected.

"Screw this. I'm going home," I said, pushing past the boys in my hurry to get out of there. Nathan followed me, so I sped up, but he caught up with me easily.

"You okay?"

"I just don't like… any of that." I didn't know how to deal with any of the feelings that had rushed to the surface.

Nathan rubbed his temples. "I'm sorry about tonight. I thought things would be different."

I shrugged. "Doesn't matter." I really wanted to go back to how it had been when we danced together, before he went cold on me. That wasn't right either—I knew there was something there. I saw it in his eyes.

"Why is everything always so intense between us?" I asked him.

"What do you mean?"

"Don't tell me you didn't feel anything back there." I stopped walking and stood in front of him.

His eyes softened. "Of course I felt… something."

"But there's *always* something, and you *always* back off! Then there are the dreams. In the art room that day, you were acting like you have *my* kind of dreams. Like it means something. What does it mean, Nathan?" I knew there was something. I felt it. I just couldn't get a firm hold on what it could be. I was determined to find out.

He shook his head. "Nothing important."

I glared up at him, but he was just as freaked out as me; I could see it in his face. I wasn't sure how to continue the conversation, so I chickened out and fell silent instead. I didn't know how to ask him questions without sounding crazy. Even though I was sure he understood exactly what I meant.

"I'm sorry everything is so messed up. I thought tonight would be fun for both of us." He said. "I want… I'm sorry."

"You can't keep stepping away at the last second," I said. He looked me right in the eye and nodded in agreement. That gave me a spark of hope that I wasn't going mad, and there really was something I didn't know yet.

"Can't we just… forget the bad stuff and remember we had a good time for a while?" His voice sounded small and vulnerable.

"What do you want from me?" I said, braver than usual.

"Everything," he whispered. "But I can't take it. I can't do that to you."

I fought the sudden lump in my throat. "I don't know what that means."

"Trust me. You're better off," he said, his voice catching. I was appalled by the look on his face, as though everything in his life was broken somehow. He bowed his head, unable to look me in the eye.

"Nathan, are you okay?" I didn't think. I just stepped toward him and held on, my forehead touching his. I gasped as his pain rolled over me. "Oh my God," I whispered as it kept coming at me, over and over, a sea of misery.

"I'm sorry," he said, pushing me away. "I forgot you feel it too."

For a split second, I gaped at him, trying to understand what he was saying, how I was feeling, and how he knew. Or how I knew for that matter.

"What is that?" I said, confused and a little scared. "What's happening to me?"

"I swear to you. It's for your own good—and mine—if we walk away right now and forget about this," he said, but every word just pushed a new wave of sadness over me. I laughed a little, feeling as if I had won something, because now I knew at least one thing for sure.

"You don't mean that," I said, hearing the incredulity in my own voice, because the certainty I had couldn't be possible. He shook his head at me, panic etched on his face. I got in his way before he had a chance to run off.

"Talk to me," I said, my palms on his chest. An imaginary fire burned through my skin, so I pushed harder and felt it run right through me. He panted like he had been sprinting. I slipped a hand to his cheek and felt the heat again. His eyes were dazed as he mumbled my name. The misery drifted away.

I hesitated, then thought screw it, I have to know, and gripped his shirt, lifting myself onto my tippy toes to reach his lips. I kissed him softly and moved away, but he held on and looked into my eyes. Then he kissed me. My fingers wound in his hair, and the kiss became fierce, passionate, never-ending. He whispered my name against my lips and held me as though he was never going to let go.

Until a low, rumbling growl separated us.

Chapter Eleven

One second I was in the middle of the best kiss of all time, the next I was behind Nathan. An enormous grey dog stood in the middle of the road, growling and baring its teeth. Impossibly large and stocky, it snapped its jaws until I grabbed the back of Nathan's shirt in alarm.

"That's a little like the dog that was outside my house." I tried to keep my voice steady—I wasn't afraid of dogs, but this one was larger than the wolfhounds and ten times as intimidating.

"Run, Perdita," Nathan whispered, staring at the dog.

"Why?" I said, but I hadn't stopped trembling since I laid eyes on the animal.

"It's not a dog." His voice was different, gruffer or something. He was right. It looked more like a timber wolf than a dog. That made no sense. I inched backward, seeing the animal joined by a smaller version that looked just as vicious—except this one had the colouring of a Golden Labrador. Maybe someone was breeding dogs with wolves?

Nathan swore, startling me. He whirled around and grabbed my hand.

"Run. Now." His eyes flashed black, they had dilated so much. He ran, pulling me along. I raced after him, trying to keep up, not even sure where we were going. I heard a howl in the distance, but when I glanced behind me, it was clear it hadn't come from either animal.

They ran after us, the grey in front, snarling and snapping ferociously. Nathan pushed me ahead of him before they caught up.

"Keep running until you get to my house," he panted. "I'm right behind you. Just trust me!" He shouted the last few words, seeing me open my mouth in protest.

I felt his fear and ran. A hot burst of adrenalin, and the idea the animals were snapping at my heels spurred me on. Minutes away from Nathan's front door, I didn't stop running, not even when Cúchulainn sprinted past me, barking like crazy.

Byron raced out of the front door, pulling his shirt open. I heard the rip as I turned around to point toward Nathan. I looked back at Byron, trying to explain, but he was gone. A huge black furry creature sped past me, almost knocking me over as it kicked out its back legs to rid itself of some shredded denim.

Baffled, I stumbled backward, internally freaking out while some wolfhounds and what looked like a smaller, whiter version of the original wolf-dog raced by me. My legs buckled beneath me. Something in my head was shouting at me to understand, but logic battened down and wouldn't let me process the thought properly.

"It's okay," a voice murmured as a pair of strong hands lifted me up. More howling rose up, louder than before, and dog barking. Lots and lots of dog barking. I looked up, speechless, into the dark brown eyes of Lia Evans—an elderly grandmother who had just lifted me from the ground with ease.

"What... what's happening?" I said, but I couldn't hear myself.

"We have to get inside," she said, her arms around me, trying to lead me inside.

"Nathan," I said, suddenly panicked. I ran off. I left him. "The dogs. Or whatever. They were right behind us. He... he told me to run here for help. I have... to go back. They were big. Really big."

She shushed me. "It's okay. Byron and Jakob are with him. They'll take care of it. You have to get inside now, okay? I'll help you. But please don't scream. I don't want Amelia to hear you."

Jakob?

My mind and body wouldn't connect. I knew I had to move, but my legs wouldn't obey. The barking died down. Lia half carried me into her house, speaking to me all the time in a language I couldn't understand. I didn't realise I was shaking until she put a blanket around my shoulders and handed me a cup of hot coffee.

"It's not possible," I said as my mind went over what had happened outside. Byron had been running toward me one second, I looked away, and he was gone, replaced by a huge dog. Not a dog. Nathan said it himself. A wolf? Wolves? In Ireland?

My face scrunched up. Lia sat next to me, waiting patiently. I opened my mouth to ask her a question, but Nathan rushed into the room, closely followed by Cúchulainn. The dog ran straight over to me.

Nathan's cheeks were flushed and his eyes excited; he didn't look scared at all, so I felt stupid. Shaking over a couple of dogs.

"You okay?" he asked me.

I nodded and looked him over. No injuries. Nathan and his grandmother exchanged glances.

"What just happened?" I said, gathering myself together.

Nathan hesitated. "Just some strays. Cú chased them off."

Lia laughed. "I think the time for that is over, Nathan."

He scowled at her but didn't speak. Jakob and Byron came into the room, the same excitement in Jakob's eyes. Byron was as cold as ever, his steely gaze fixed on me.

"You changed clothes," I said, half to myself as a part of my awareness found a tidbit in my memory that I needed to focus upon. When I first saw him, he was wearing jeans and a shirt, now he had on a loose tracksuit—as if he was about to go jogging. He had ripped open his shirt. I knew it didn't make sense at the time, but I was too worried about Nathan to quite grasp what he was doing. I looked around, and he was gone. Not gone. Not exactly.

"*You*... changed."

I said the words; I couldn't take them back, no matter how much my brain wanted me to. Byron was the black creature. He had turned into the black creature. Not a dog.

"Wolf?" I whispered, looking at Nathan. He looked as though he might vomit.

The atmosphere in the room tightened. "Wolf." I said again, more sure of myself. Nathan wouldn't look at me. Nobody denied it or said I was crazy. Nobody laughed. They should have laughed. It made no sense. I sounded insane.

"It had to be done sometime," Lia said. "It's true then. They're here?" She looked at her husband.

Jakob sat next to her and put his arm around her shoulders. She leaned into him, sighing heavily.

"They ran," Byron said. "No danger. Coincidence even."

"What's happening here?" I said. "Where's Amelia? Somebody tell me... something. Something that makes sense."

Lia took my hand and patted it, but it wasn't until Nathan moved closer to me that I felt better.

"Opa," he said. "I can't..."

Byron paced the room and then halted, looking right at me. "She saw. It's done. Perdita, yes, I changed into a wolf. I'm known as a werewolf, I suppose."

I laughed, close to hysterical. A buzzing in my head kept getting louder and louder. I had to raise my voice just to hear myself. "Werewolves. Amelia's bracelet. All this time, she's been hinting, and I thought she was off her head. Where is she?"

"Asleep," Lia said. "She doesn't need to hear about this."

"She doesn't know?"

Lia smiled. "She knows, but she doesn't need to worry about other werewolves."

"Other... werewolves?"

"You were chased by werewolves, but we're not certain why. We don't know them. We ran them off. They probably won't be back." Byron's voice was brisk, unfeeling.

"There's more of them," I said. They all stared at me. "At least one. I saw it outside my house one night. There was a dead cat on my doorstep the next day. But the... wolf, it wasn't the same colour as those ones tonight." I looked at Nathan, tried to see something in his face. Staring at his clothes, I realised he hadn't been wearing them before.

"You? Are... you?"

He wouldn't look at me, and I had my answer. I tried to imagine him as a wolf, but the buzzing got louder, and my world turned upside down. Lia held my head on my knees and told me to breathe. Her voice sounded funny in my head, echoing. After a few minutes of keeping my head down and trying to understand what everyone was whispering, I found it easier to breathe and pushed Lia's hands away.

"Wow," I said. "I have to go home. I can't be late."

I stood, still shaking, still unable to take in any of it. Jakob took my hands.

"It's going to be all right, Perdita. I'll drive you home now, but we can talk about this again," he said, but then he spoke more sternly. "But you must never speak of this to anyone else. Do you understand?"

I saw darkness in his eyes, but I nodded, wanting to get away. Needing to get away.

"Wait," Nathan said. "I need to talk to her first."

Jakob hesitated, but Lia laid a hand on his arm. "Give them a minute. Nathan, take Cú."

Nathan took my hand and led me outside, followed by Cúchulainn. I wanted to pull my hand away, but when he touched me, I felt a little better than before. Did he have some kind of magical power over me? My whole body went numb, but my mind kept racing, throwing the same few sentences out, over and over again.

Nothing came out of my mouth. Not when he faced me. Not when he called my name. He held me close to him, and I slowly felt better.

"Is that some kind of werewolf thing?" I asked.

"Is what some kind of werewolf thing?" he mumbled against my hair.

"Making me feel better when you touch me. That's a thing, right?"

He sighed. "That's a thing."

"Is that why everyone likes you?"

"What?"

I swallowed. "Everyone likes you. Is that why? You're doing something to them?"

"No, I'm not doing anything to them except trying to fit in." Something in his voice made me think I was asking the wrong question.

"Is it... why *I* like you? Is there something you're doing to me?"

He hesitated, his arms pulling me tighter. "Yes."

I pushed him away and took a few deep breaths.

"I'm sorry," he said at last.

"For what?"

"For... everything. There's a lot I have to tell you now, and it's all, well, it's pretty much just as bizarre as everything else tonight. My family is cursed, and you're a part of it."

"Me?" I blinked a couple of times. "How? Is this all a joke or something?"

He shook his head. "No joke. We can talk about it sometime. After you've had a chance to let it sink in."

I nodded. "Yeah. Yeah, that would probably be the best thing to do. Except, why were they chasing us? Those other... you know."

He shrugged. "Not sure. They weren't exactly friendly, but they ran off pretty quick."

"Are you dangerous?" I blurted out.

"I'm not going to hurt you," he said firmly. "Take Cú with you if you're scared. You know he'll protect you."

I laughed, but it sounded small and shaky. "Don't think Dad would approve. I really have to go."

None of us spoke in the car. I squashed myself as far into the corner of the seat as I could. Jakob hummed along to the radio as though there was nothing at all strange about the world.

I made it home in time. Nathan walked me to my door but didn't put his hands on me at all. I was grateful because I felt as though I were about to burst out of my skin, and I didn't need him doing whatever he kept doing to take away what I was really feeling. He put his hands in his pockets and looked almost ashamed, as though he knew exactly what I was thinking.

"I'll see you tomorrow?" he asked, but he sounded unsure.

"Maybe. I don't know yet."

He nodded and waited until I got inside. I watched the car pull away even though Dad was still up.

"You got a lift?"

"Yeah, um, Nathan's grandfather drove me home because he was worried."

"Worried?"

I rubbed my eyes. "Yeah, he thinks it's as dangerous here as everywhere else. I'm off to bed, okay? I'm exhausted. Too much dancing."

He smiled. "Well, I hope you enjoyed yourself."

I plastered a smile on my face. "Of course."

Upstairs, I lay on my bed and found it hard to breathe. Nothing made sense to me. Nathan kissed me—I curled up with pleasure at that memory. But then a dog came. Except it wasn't a dog. It was a wolf. No, not even a wolf. A werewolf. A myth come true. And Nathan was one too.

I kissed Nathan.

I kissed a werewolf.

The thought was confusing more than repulsive. I didn't freak out at the idea of Nathan changing into an animal, or even the notion he might be able to change how I felt with his touch—but the idea he might never have told me was... bothersome. Worse still, what did the other werewolves want?

I had always wanted *something* to happen, but I hadn't meant this.

Chapter Twelve

A black shaggy werewolf visited my dreams all night. Hunted by others, over and over. I woke in the middle of the night, gasping for air, still struggling to make sense of everything. I wasn't sure of anything anymore. Lucky it was Sunday—school would have been hell.

I hung around my house, only speaking to Joey briefly. I tried to sound normal, but I doubt he would have noticed anyway; he and Tammie had gotten together at the party. Tammie didn't call or text me at all to tell me about it, but in a way, it was a relief, my head was too messed up to talk to her.

I thought over what I knew. It wasn't much. I liked Nathan. I knew there was something different about him, but a werewolf? That wouldn't have dawned on me in a million years. Even now I found it hard to believe, despite seeing a couple of wolves.

That niggled at me. What did they want? They picked an awkward time to attack. Right when Nathan and I kissed. At the time, it felt like they were warning me away, reminding me of the way Cú had warned Nathan when he accidentally hurt me.

I sat alone in my living room for hours until Lia Evans knocked at my door. I wasn't sure I even wanted to open it, but my head buzzed with questions. Maybe she could help me. I invited her in, suddenly nervous around her.

"How are you feeling today?" she asked, looking me over carefully.

I shrugged. She gave a little sigh and sat down. "There's more you need to know. I hope this isn't too soon. If you need more time..."

More? What else could there be? Wasn't the fact werewolves existed enough? But I had to know. "I'd rather be told, thanks. *Seeing* impossible things happen is a bit of a shock, you know?"

She smiled, but her eyes were sad. "There was nobody around to tell me these things," she said. "I was older than you when I met my Jakob. I was already a believer—in a lot of ways—but it was still a shock. The whole story. It's a big deal."

"A shock? Aren't you one too?"

"Now I am," she said. "My choice, don't worry."

I couldn't hide my horror.

"It's not that bad," she said softly. "Not always. I'm here for Nathan. He couldn't tell you… everything. But you need to know, so here I am."

"Need to know what now?"

"Everything. You haven't asked questions yet. I thought you would. There's a story behind it all, and you're a part of it."

"Me? How?"

"My husband isn't the first in his family to become a werewolf. In fact, the first was in the 18th century. The story is that he was bitten by a wolf and changed suddenly—unable to control himself, he attacked a Romani Gypsy camp and slaughtered the favourite daughter of an elder. They cursed him and his pregnant wife to suffer. They would have one child, a son, cursed to become a werewolf and wander the earth in search of his soul mate, one who would make him happy. Each generation would follow the same path, turn into a werewolf on their 16th birthday, and look for their mate. The curse would only be broken when a daughter was born."

She looked at me meaningfully. "Okay," I said. "That makes no sense."

Lia laughed. "This time yesterday, you probably would have said the same thing if someone told you Nathan's a werewolf."

I stared at her, knowing she was right.

"Things changed," she said. "I became a werewolf by choice and gave birth to twin sons, the first time since the curse that more than one child was born. We think that my choice made the difference. Things went normally for Byron, he had one son. But Luis, my other boy, he and his wife had a second child, Amelia. A girl. The first in the family in centuries. The one supposed to break the curse. Except it didn't happen. Nathan turned last year, and he's been looking for his mate ever since. You."

I stared at her, waiting for her to laugh. "That's a joke, right?"

"I'm sorry, Perdita. I know it's a lot to take in. But you *are* Nathan's mate. You're cursed too. I remember what it was like. I dreamt of Jakob for a year before we met. Whenever he was near me, I felt good, well, better. I sensed his emotions and knew how to make him happy on instinct. I couldn't keep away from him, no matter how hard I tried, and once we gave in to the curse, it was beautiful."

Most of what she described could apply to me too. It was getting too creepy. Soul mates? I didn't believe in that sort of thing. Then again, I didn't believe in werewolves either.

"Nathan's always said he would fight the curse. And he has, I suppose. He didn't want to tell you any of this. He wanted you to have a chance. But we can't fight the curse and win, none of us. It's better if you give in, and let it take its course." She held my hands in hers and nodded at me.

"No," I said, too loud. "I'm not… I have a mind. Free will. I'm not going to just… change everything I believe in because you tell me I'm cursed."

"It's okay, Perdita. I know what you're going through. Trust me. But the curse is strong. strong enough to make you feel good around him. Designed to make you feel bereft away from him. It's made to last."

Lia let that sink in. The curse was really screwing me over.

"The thing is," she said, hesitating a little. "We keep away from others like us. Very few shifters can breed like we do. It's an important part of our heritage. Some werewolves out there believe the males in my family should always mate in a werewolf, to produce more werewolves—like I did. And then there are those who don't want the curse to end at all, so we've kept Amelia… safe. If she's meant to end the curse then she needs to stay well."

"Amelia's not safe?" My heart pounded in my chest. I hated the thought of those animals getting near her. They would tear her apart.

Lia shook her head. "I'm not saying that; we're just being careful because of… things that happened in the past. We were probably overly cautious, but I need you to play down what happened with the werewolves last night. I don't want to scare her unnecessarily. She's not a shifter. She doesn't need to be involved in any of this."

I exhaled loudly. Something in Lia's face worried me. "Is that it?" I asked.

"There's lots I can tell you, but maybe we'll stick to one big revelation a day, yes?" She smiled at me, but I couldn't return it, I felt too sick inside.

"How about you spend the day with my family and see how normal we are? I know Amelia would love to see you. She was so disappointed about missing the party last night."

"Good thing she did miss it," I said, but I wanted to see her too.

This time I asked Dad if I could go. He agreed—after he spoke to Lia on the phone. I needed to speak to Nathan, yet after the whole soul mate thing, I didn't really know what I should say to him. Nothing in life had prepared me for this kind of crazy supernatural deal.

At her home, Lia made a fuss over me—as did Jakob. Byron merely nodded at me. I had a feeling he wouldn't bat an eyelid if I disintegrated in front of him. Nathan hung around a bit, but he pretty much avoided looking at me, never mind speaking to me, so when Lia asked me if I wanted to see Amelia, I jumped at the chance.

She was in bed, still sniffling. "Hey," she said, smiling when I entered the room. "Sit as close as you dare."

I laughed and sat on the edge of her bed. She pushed her e-reader aside. I took a quick peek and grinned when I saw she had been reading a popular teen romance title. Not so different after all.

"I heard you know everything about my freaky family now," she said, but she looked proud when she said it.

"I've heard one or two things all right." I made a face.

"You're not happy?" Surprise raised her voice a pitch.

"Happy? Of course I'm not happy! There's all this stuff going on that apparently involves me, but not one of you came out and told me until you had no choice anymore. I thought *you* were my friend. And Nathan?" I shook my head, unable to speak.

"It's not my story to tell. He's my brother, Perdita. I couldn't do that to him if he wasn't ready. I told you the truth before. He's a coward. He was afraid of you long before he met you. I suppose it's scary, knowing your future is already mapped out for you."

"No, I can't accept that. I won't. I know this whole curse thing is what your family is about, but not me. I mean, how do you all know I'm his, you know, anyway?"

Amelia yawned. "He knew. The first day he saw you. He never said anything, but I guessed when I saw you two together, and part of me already knew too. I might not be a werewolf or a soul mate, but I'm part of this. Me and you are connected too, just in a smaller way. I knew when I saw you that we would be friends. It just seemed perfect when it turned out you might be Nathan's mate."

"Might," I repeated.

She made a scornful noise. "Too late for maybes. Even the dogs know."

That confused me.

"Don't you get it?" she said, laughing. "My family has always had wolfhounds, ever since the first werewolf. They run with us, protect us, protect the mates. Cú is Nathan's dog, but as soon as he saw you, you became his number one. He protected you, even against Nathan. He knows it's you."

"The *dog* knows about me?" Even after everything, I was sceptical.

"It's not that he knows, like he can talk or anything. It's more like… you're part of his pack, and he's responsible for you."

"That's weird."

"What part of this isn't?" she said with a huge grin.

"So how does it work?"

"I mean, nobody knows for sure or anything but, apparently, the curse is the only one of its kind in the whole world. That shows how powerful it is. Isn't that amazing?" Her eyes lit up.

I grimaced. "No, not really. So none of this is real then? How I feel, I mean. Am I his only choice? If you had moved somewhere different, would he have found someone else… qualified?"

She chuckled then gave a little cough. "I'm not positive, but I don't think that's how it works. I believe there's just one in the world for him. I mean, Byron's wife died, and he hasn't met anyone else."

"That's so sad," I said, horrified. "Can't he just be with someone who isn't his mate?"

She shook her head, looking grave. "It would never feel even close to the same thing."

"Is that why Nathan pulls away from me? Because it'll ruin how he'll feel for anyone else?" I bit my lip.

"No, of course not. He's just scared of dragging you into all of this."

"Bit late for that, no?"

"But Perdy, it isn't just you. He has this thing about bringing his own son out hunting." She shrugged as if she didn't know what the problem was.

"Hunting? Does he… eat people or something?"

"No!" she said, shocked. "That's not… he doesn't do anything like that. My family would never hurt anyone."

I chewed this over. "Is it a full moon thing?"

"Nah, that's not true." She looked at me scornfully. As if I knew what could be possible or not.

"So why do they change at all? If they don't have to."

She scrunched up her face, thinking hard. "They do, kinda. To stay healthy, they have to change and hunt every now and then. Just small animals though, it's more about the exercise, I think. It's like they get really edgy if they don't let the wolf out every now and then."

I exhaled loudly. "And Nathan does this? Changes. Goes hunting?"

"Yeah," she said. "But he's Nathan. You know him. He's still the same person."

"Except he gets a bit furry every now and then."

"It's not his fault," she protested.

I looked at her seriously. "I know."

We sat in silence for a couple of minutes while I let it all sink in. I felt as if I was in a dream world and expected to wake up from it any second. I kept waiting, but it didn't happen. This was my life.

I looked at Amelia shyly. "What does he look like? You know, as a werewolf?"

She giggled. "Oh, he's huge. Long black hair. Definitely an improvement."

"Hmm. I think I dreamt about him. As a werewolf, I mean. That's weird, right?"

"That's normal for us. Anyway, it's good you know. We can talk about everything. No secrets; you and Nathan can be together and be happy now. Everything's worked out!"

"What are you talking about?" I was baffled by her attitude. "Nothing's worked out! This is all… messed up. Beyond messed up. I'm not happy, and Nathan doesn't exactly look thrilled either. Why couldn't he tell me all of this himself, anyway?"

"Told you. Coward. Don't you see how lucky you are? You know exactly who in this world will make you happy, and you know for sure they feel the same way. It's amazing."

I couldn't believe what she was saying to me. Amazing? To have no choice? To be cursed? I wanted the truth, but now I was cursed with it. I finally had the truth I looked for, but my brain wouldn't let me understand it. I needed to talk to Nathan. He was the only one I wanted to talk to about it all. It was about me and him; we were the only ones who could discuss it.

"I need to talk to him, Amelia. I can't... I just have to hear it from him. Why won't he talk to me?"

"He's scared. I keep telling you. Just leave him be. He'll be ready sometime."

"He wasn't ever going to tell me any of this, was he?" He looked so disappointed when I found out that I knew it could have been his secret for always if it was left up to him.

"It's not that. I mean, he would have eventually. The curse wouldn't let him avoid you forever—but he's been the one who wants to fight it. He's always said as much. He can't hack it really." She looked embarrassed, as though he was the family shame. That made me even madder.

"I'm going to speak to him right now," I said and marched out of the room. I wasn't sure where I got the balls from, but I walked right up to him in front of his whole family.

"We need to talk. Now."

Nathan stuttered and looked around at his grandparents helplessly.

"Oh, no you don't," I said. "You don't get to run away. You're going to talk me this time."

I grabbed his arm and pulled him outside, noticing a small smile on Byron's face as we passed him by. I led Nathan to the swings, but once he knew I was serious, he followed me without struggling.

I sat on a swing, rocking idly.

"This is mad," I said. He nodded but didn't say a word. "They told me about the soul mate thing. Why didn't you?"

"How was I supposed to bring it up? Hey Perdita, wanna go out with me? By the way, we're destined to be together forever, and oh, yeah, you're going to mother my werewolf son."

I laughed out loud. I couldn't help it. "Sweet of you and all, but I'm not planning on starting a family any time soon." I stopped the swing. "Did you expect someone better? Are you sulking because I'm what the curse came up with?"

"That's the stupidest thing I've ever heard," he muttered.

"I'm stupid now?"

"No, you just said something stupid. Bet they didn't tell you all of it." He mumbled something and walked off. I ran after him.

"Yeah, they did! They told me you're cursed. You're a werewolf. You're supposed to find your soul mate. I'm it, so happy ever freaking after! Except you've done your best to avoid me, so it can't be that big a deal, and who says I want any part of this anyway!"

He swung around, his eyes looked black again. "You don't know everything. That much is obvious." He kept walking, away from his house, and away from me.

"You don't get to keep running away," I shouted after him.

"Then come with me," he called back. So I did.

"All of these places are empty," he said, pointing at the houses neighbouring his own. "That's partly why we moved here. Nobody to hear us howl. Nobody to wonder why they're suddenly inundated with wolves. Come on."

He passed through the gate of one of the houses, jumped on a bin, and climbed in through a broken window. He stuck his head out and grinned at me, waiting. I clambered onto the bin, feeling stupid, and let him help me inside.

"We'll get into trouble for being here," I said, mostly to distract myself from the way my stomach fluttered when he touched me.

He shrugged. "What are they gonna do? Put a collar on me? Relax, nobody comes around here. Not much anyway."

He took my hand again and showed me around. The place was filthy. One of the rooms had an old mattress on the floor and some upturned crates. I sat on the cleanest one I could find. A sudden ray of light beamed through the dirty window, giving the place a creepy colour. Nathan pulled a crate in front of mine and sat facing me.

"I'm sorry, okay? But I didn't ask for any of this. I'm the one who turns into a wolf, so I think I've come off the worst here, don't you? I hate this curse thing. I thought it was over. It was supposed to be—Amelia was born. But then last year, I suddenly turned into a wolf. I thought I was dying or something; it was horrible. I swore I would fight this curse and not drag anyone down with me."

"Why?" I said. "What's so bad about it?"

"For one, I don't want to inflict this crap on my own kid. For another, I never wanted to doom some girl to this. They didn't tell you everything. I should have known they wouldn't. The gypsies cursed my family to suffer, and the only way to truly suffer is to truly love. The curse is to suffer while you look for the soul mate. You find her and experience true love and happiness, but then she's taken away. It always ends in tragedy." He looked at me with sad eyes. "The soul mate always dies, Perdita. Always. Too soon. We outlive our mates, so we can mourn their deaths."

I shook my head. "That's not true; your grandmother's still here."

"Maybe that's 'cos she's a wolf too, I don't know. But it's the only time it's ever worked out. Byron's wife died really suddenly—cancer—and my mother…" Nathan took a deep breath. "My Dad probably killed her. Accidentally, maybe, but still."

"What?" I hadn't expected that revelation.

"They found her body. Killed by a wild animal, or so they said. He was gone. Never came back. She was killed by a werewolf, and he vanished—it's more than likely that he killed her. He loved her. Trust me, he really loved her. If he could do that… so could I."

I shook my head again, refusing to believe. "You wouldn't. There has to be an explanation."

"Yeah, he probably lost control. It happens. If we get angry, really angry, sometimes we lose control and shift without meaning to. Their dog died a week before, so there was nobody looking out for my mother when it happened. If I did that—to you, to anyone—I wouldn't be able to deal with it, okay?" His voice broke then, his shoulders shook, and I was before him, holding on, feeling his pain slam into me.

"It's okay," I said, stroking his hair. "Nothing bad is going to happen."

We stayed like that for a while, not talking, just holding on. His family didn't understand him at all. Amelia kept calling him a coward, but really, he had too much heart. Too much lost and still to lose. Eventually, his pain subsided, and I felt red-hot heat instead. Blushing, I backed away and sat on my crate again.

"Is it just the curse?" I asked. "If it broke, would we… hate each other or something?"

"No way of knowing," he said, holding my gaze. "It's powerful. It makes us feel good when we're together and bad when we're apart. It lets us feel each other's emotions. Lets us really connect so we'll be attracted to each other. Once we give in, it's supposed to be the best feeling ever."

"And then we have a kid," I said, pouring cold water on his words.

"Apparently," he said, looking at his hands.

"So what if we just… didn't do anything that makes a baby."

He flushed red. "If it was that simple then someone would have done it by now, right? Byron couldn't explain it properly, but he said you lose your mind a little. That everything reaches a point where you can't help yourself."

"I *really* think I can control myself," I said, biting my lip. "Besides, I'm not sure I even want a kid when I'm older."

"Easy to say now," he reminded me. "You've another twenty or thirty years to change your mind."

"Or maybe we'll figure out how to stop the thing altogether."

"Well, that'll make it easier to resist you," he said, then startled me by kneeling in front of me and just looking at me.

"I've been trying not to stare at you for too long since the first time I saw you. I've been holding everything in so you wouldn't feel it. Can I just… be me for a while?"

I felt my cheeks burn under his gaze. I nodded slowly, feeling as though we were doing something dangerous. "Maybe for a while, but then we have to think about this. I like you, but maybe I don't know you. Maybe we should be taking things slow, like normal people, and not worry about what some curse has in store for us."

He smiled then leaned closer to me, his face inches away from mine. He put his hands on my arms and slowly ran his fingers up to my shoulders. I held my breath as he touched his nose to my cheek and inhaled deeply. It was strange, if I thought about it; if I didn't, it felt right.

He touched my hair and gazed at me again, so close without doing anything more than touch me lightly. I felt frantic inside, wondering what my life was going to lead to. I didn't love him, barely knew him, yet all of these people thought my life was with him.

I held his face in my hands and felt his breathing quicken as I kissed him. Slower than before, on the street when we had been in a mad panic. We took our time, testing ourselves, seeing what it felt like when we both knew everything. I saw how easy it would be to lose my mind a little. It never occurred to me to walk away from him or to be scared because of what he told me. I felt as though I really knew what he was made of, and it wasn't anything bad.

We stayed there, barely talking, just being close to each other until the sky darkened, and I got cold.

"I should probably go home," I said. He kissed me, pulling me closer to him, and my skin electrified; it was as if my body didn't want to leave. I pushed him away, laughing to cover how shaky I felt. "Really, I should go."

"I know." He looked me over and brushed my hair from my face. "I bet I wouldn't hate you if there wasn't a curse."

I looked into his eyes and half-believed him. This time I pushed against him, holding his face, twisting my fingers in his hair as I gave him one last lingering kiss. In his arms, I felt as if I belonged there. But the world was waiting for us to return, and I knew we couldn't keep hiding in empty houses just to figure life out.

When we pulled apart, his expression was serious. "Taking our time?"

"Starting now," I said, grinning. "We get to know each other. See if maybe we can figure out a way around all this stuff."

"And then what?" He looked worried.

"We decide. Not curses or werewolves or our families. Just us."

"When did you get to be so sensible?" He nuzzled at my neck.

"I don't know. Maybe I learned it from my Dad."

"You never talk about your mother," he said.

"You never talk about werewolves!"

"Touché. Come on. I'll walk you home." He helped me up, but I couldn't resist sliding my arms around his neck one last time.

On the way home, we walked side by side, as close as we dared. Despite the blissful mood, I felt as though I had to talk about werewolves.

"Will Amelia change? It happens when you're sixteen, right?"

"I have no idea. I didn't think *I* would, so anything can happen. She'd like it though. The weirdo."

"She is a little bit obsessed," I said, thinking hard. "You know, it felt as if those other werewolves were coming after us last night. Didn't you think so?"

He glanced at me, looking a little sick. "I felt like they were going after you, not me. Maybe Byron is right. Maybe it was a coincidence."

"This is a tiny place. Why would two separate groups of werewolves suddenly turn up at the same time? It's a little convenient, no?"

"He wants to avoid any confrontations. I mean, those were the first ones I've seen. Aside from my family, I mean. My cousin, Jeremy, he's come across others, but we all avoid them. We move, just to keep out of their way. Or rather, to keep Amelia out of their way. I don't know why really. I mean, nothing's happened to us."

"Funny timing. Right when we kiss, they show up."

"Suppose. Maybe you really should take Cúchulainn."

"He'd pine for home," I scoffed. "Besides, remember my Dad? Big man who says no?"

"He'd say yes for me," Nathan said with a grin. "Cú is protective of you now. He'll do his job. No matter what."

"Would he obey me?"

"Sure. Perdita, what's the story with us? What are we going to tell people?"

"Do we have to tell them anything?" I looked up at him hopefully.

"Depends on if there is anything to tell, right? I mean, if we're just friends then..."

I laughed out loud at the look on his face. "What do you want to do?"

"I don't really care as long as you're nearby, to be honest." He stopped and put his hands on my shoulders. "It was okay before, you know? I could tell myself I was protecting you. That it was for your own good. But now I've gotten a taste... it's harder to let go."

I was shocked by the intensity behind his words; he let me feel his emotions, and they made me want to take him by the hand and run away with him.

"I don't know what to do," I said. "I mean, we don't want a kid, and we definitely don't want a curse telling us what to do. I'm cool, sort of, with the werewolf thing, but I don't want to be the tragic ending. So how do we beat it?"

"We'll figure something out. I promise. I'm not going to let anything happen to you. As for the other stuff, we don't have to... do anything, so don't worry. I still want to fight the curse, but I feel stronger when you're with me so that's a bit of a contradiction, right?"

"We'll fix it," I said, and we both ignored the obvious. We didn't have a clue how to fix anything.

Chapter Thirteen

That night, I lay on my bed, thinking hard. Everything was changing so fast that I felt as if I couldn't catch my breath. Nathan. Werewolf. His family. Werewolves. Me. His soul mate? It sounded like something out of a cheesy novel, but there I was, living it. The weirdest part was how much sense it made to me. As though I already knew it and had just forgotten.

My biggest question turned out to be why me? Of everyone in the world, why was I the one he was cursed to look for? It made no sense. He ended up in the tiny little place I lived. I was his sister's best friend. I had felt a connection to both of them straight away. But why?

I pondered this question more than any other. I found I had no trouble believing in werewolves, but believing myself to be the soul mate was something else altogether. If I had a child with him, it would be a werewolf. How was that possible? Did I have some weird genetic disposition that made me susceptible? What was it that picked *me*?

I tormented myself way into the night but came up with no answers. So I moved on to how things would change between us. Being alone together had been electrifying. I wondered how much of that was the curse, rather than our real feelings. I couldn't even trust my own body anymore. I never worried in the heat of the moment, but later on, alone and cold, I couldn't help the doubts that flooded my mind.

The following morning, he and I were alone together on the bus. At first I felt shy but, ever so slowly, I got the sense that he was mine, and as he already knew I was supposed to have feelings for him, it didn't seem so bad. There was no point feeling awkward now everything was out in the open.

"How are you?" he said, looking at me with something akin to fear in his eyes. I squeezed his hand and liked that he didn't pull away.

"Still trying to make sense of stuff. You?"

He looked surprised. "I feel good, actually. Didn't think I would. We can't really talk much. In public, I mean. About… stuff. But I wanted to tell you, if you want to walk away, I'll understand. This stuff is crazy. I get that, and I don't expect you to just jump into anything because we told you that you have no choice."

I couldn't help smiling at him. "We talked about this yesterday. No big decisions. We're taking it slow and trying to figure out a loophole or something. Maybe we can figure out what Amelia is supposed to do."

"And if we can't?" He raised an eyebrow.

"We'll deal with it when we're old enough for it to be a problem."

For some reason that made him grin. "What?" I said, shy again.

"You're already bossing me around," he teased, squeezing my knee.

I pushed him away, laughing. "You're lucky Cú isn't around."

"The traitor. Wanna do something later?"

That cheered me up. "Of course."

"How about I call for you after school?"

I agreed, and we spent the rest of the journey acting as though there were no werewolves at all.

***

"Where's Amelia?" Tammie's tone was a little snappy at lunch-time.

"Still sick," I said, looking around for Nathan.

"Did you have a good time on Saturday?" Joey kept fidgeting with his watch, unusually restless.

"It was… interesting," I said, not referring to the party at all.

"Yeah, well, *we* had a great time, didn't we Joe?" Tammie pushed her chair closer to his. He didn't look as enthusiastic.

"Good," I said, wondering why she was glaring at me. Nathan sat next to me and rested his arm around the back of my chair. He didn't touch me, but we both grinned at each other. It was such a relief now I didn't have to worry if he liked me or if I was just imagining it. I had to thank the curse for that one thing.

Nathan and Joey chatted together pleasantly enough, but Tammie had a face like thunder.

"Are you okay?" I asked after a couple of minutes of watching her glare in our direction.

"You two together?" she snapped.

Nathan and I looked at each other, both speechless and unsure of how to answer.

"Because if you are, we got there first."

All three of us stared at Tammie in disbelief. "Um," I said. "What?"

"Don't think you can copy us. I mean it." She stood and stalked off.

"Joey?" I said. "What was that about?" I was getting very tired of Tammie's irrational mood-swings.

He shook his head wearily. "I have no idea." Then his expression turned stern. "*Are* you with each other now?"

I looked at Nathan again. "We're just… taking it slow. Getting to know each other. You?"

Joey shrugged. "Ask the boss lady."

I laughed, but all of a sudden I didn't find anything funny.

I forgot about Tammie's weird attitude for the last few classes because I spent my time wondering what Nathan and I were going to do later on. He sat next to me most of the day, and I could see Dawn getting more and more annoyed, but I was too excited to care. For once, everything seemed exciting.

After school, I walked from the bus-stop to my house, feeling good. But as I approached my own home, I noticed two figures loitering outside. Getting closer, I recognised them both. The red-haired man with amber eyes leaned against my wall; the blonde woman stood close by, glaring in my direction.

I moved closer, my pulse quickening. Her hair colour was pretty similar to one of the wolves. His resembled the wolf I had seen outside my house. So where was the third?

The way the man looked at me made my skin crawl, and the hatred in the woman's eyes terrified me. It was wild and barely controlled, and I had no idea what I had done to make her mad.

The closer I got, the more I realised they were trying to scare me… or something. He was bad enough; That smug smirk on his lips made me want to slap him. The woman, on the other hand, reminded me of something. The same look that had been in the wolf's eye. The look that made me feel threatened, hunted… *warned*.

I closed the gate behind me, never taking my eyes off them. "Can I help you?" I said to the man, my voice as steady as I could manage.

"Not yet," he said with a grin.

I hurried to my front door and opened it before getting annoyed at the way they tried to intimidate me.

"I know what you are," I called out, feeling brave and taking a chance. By the way the man started, I had my answer. Definitely werewolves. I watched through the window and saw the man try to push the woman. She slapped his hand away and strode on ahead of him. He ran his fingers through his hair and took one last look at my house, his shoulders slumped.

By the time Nathan turned up, I was more angry than scared. I tried to explain it to him on the way to his house, but I might have been a little over-excited. He held my hand, and I felt calmer. Calm enough to speak slowly in front of Nathan's family.

"Hold on. You think these people are werewolves?" Byron's eyes narrowed.

"Yes!" I said for at least the third time. "They've been following us around. I swear. I've seen the man a couple of times, and I saw the woman staring at Nathan and Dawn one day. Think about it! Dawn said she saw a wolf—so did I! There was a dead animal on both of our doorsteps. The expression on that man's face today. It was obvious!"

Byron still looked sceptical. "You can't just go around accusing strangers of being werewolves. Why would they follow you around? More importantly, why this Dawn girl?"

I frowned. I hadn't figured that one out yet.

"I believe you," Lia said.

"No," Jakob said firmly.

"But you must remember. This is so familiar," she insisted, but his scowl made me shiver.

"Coincidence," he said. "That's all. The child is excitable; she just found out about us."

I snorted. "I am *not* excitable. Those wolves came after *me* the other night, not Nathan."

"They didn't actually hurt you. Those people today didn't actually threaten you," Byron reminded me. "And your school friend has no part in any of this."

"Maybe they don't like this soul mate thing," I said, thinking hard. "Other wolves want Nathan to be with a werewolf, right?" I looked at him for confirmation.

"This is true," Lia said, ignoring her husband's glare.

"Well, maybe they weren't sure who his soul mate was."

Jakob scoffed, but Nathan's face brightened. "She's right. Dawn's always hugging me and stuff, but Perdita keeps her distance. If a stranger was watching, they might get the wrong idea."

"So they threatened both girls with a blood sacrifice," Lia said, her voice sounding distant. "And waited to see which one he would protect. Except he doesn't know the ways. He didn't see the danger. Then they watched. She's right. They didn't know and took their chances on both girls. Until they saw Nathan with one of them for sure."

"That's enough," Jakob said. "Enough of this. We will search for them, yes. But there is no need for this panic. Do not worry the children; history never has to repeat itself."

He and Lia left the room, arguing in hushed tones. Byron looked thoughtful but not altogether worried. "As my father said, we'll take a look around. Chances are they scented us, were curious and have now been chased off. I don't see any imminent danger. No more talk of this unless something else happens, and don't scare Amelia with your stories."

He left the room, leaving me bewildered. Nathan gripped my hand.

"What's a blood sacrifice," I asked him.

"I've no idea."

For some reason, him not knowing the answer to everything made my chin tremble.

"It's okay," he said. "They won't touch you. It's too late now. We've already met. They can't stop it. If they're sticking around, then we'll know."

"Why is your family acting like this?"

"I don't know. I hate how cautious they are. I mean, it's not like I want everyone to know about us, but we're handicapped for stuff like this. We don't know how to track, or even how to defend ourselves. I need to know what's going on."

He paced up and down the room. "It's head-wrecking. If I step out of line here, Byron will forbid me from doing something, and then I'll be useless to you."

"Forbid you?"

"Yeah, like, I'll physically be unable to do what I want. He has the strongest will, so what he says goes. As soon as I'm old enough to be stronger than him, I'm totally taking the alpha from him."

I burst out laughing. "Sorry, sorry! That's just... not what I expected you to say."

He grinned back at me. "You just wait. Seriously though, it's frustrating. He's so bloody careful about everything, and I can't do a thing about it. It was okay before, but now it involves you, and I feel like I *have* to do something about it."

"He's just trying to take care of you," I said, but really I thought Byron was too civilised to be a werewolf. Thinking that other werewolves acted the same way was a mistake. I saw the look in that woman's eyes—she meant me harm. I was mentally preparing myself to be attacked, for real this time. If they moved around to keep Amelia out of the path of werewolves, then they should have prepared themselves for the worst at all times.

"Maybe I should go. Tell Amelia I was here, okay?" I said, preparing myself to leave.

"I will, but don't go yet. We can go outside, or back to that house if you want, just... hang out for a bit?"

Lia followed us outside, gesturing for us to move away from the house. "Walk with me."

She led us out of the gate and down the road, Cúchulainn at my feet.

"I want to talk to you both about a couple of things. First, this curse. Just because you're meant to be doesn't mean you have to make silly decisions. There's no hurry, so don't go rushing headfirst into anything." She stared at us until we both flushed deep red. It wasn't a subject I was comfortable discussing with Nathan's grandmother.

"Second of all, these people. I believe you, Perdita, and I think you're probably right. I'm not saying they're following you or even that they're werewolves, but I have a bad feeling. It wouldn't be the first time." She stopped talking abruptly, as if changing her mind about what she was going to say.

"What is it?" Nathan asked, but I could feel the tension rise from him.

She stopped walking and faced us. "You know we keep to ourselves, Nathan. And Perdita, you have to understand, we don't embrace the wolf. I love who I am, but I have to follow the path set by the alpha—I don't have a choice. It's something that compels the wolf, and I am wolf too. We have rules. Even if we deny ourselves the life that goes with it."

"Okay," I said, unsure where she was going with it.

She took a deep breath. "Just because I follow the set path doesn't mean I agree with it. I want to know more about what we are. About our heritage and other shifters. We might have figured this out by now. We've run away too many times. I don't believe we're going to find those people. Not if they're werewolves. They know better than us how to hide their tracks, so I'm going to keep looking until I know for sure. I'm not going to let anything happen to any of you."

Her eyes dilated like Nathan's. "I'm with you," he said.

She nodded, and a fleeting moment passed between them. She looked proud, but a part of me was sad that she seemed surprised by it.

"Go," she said. "Have fun. Be young. But be careful, and let me know if anything happens. Speak to me first, always."

She hurried away, but I stopped her.

"Wait," I said. "Can I ask you some questions?"

She nodded, surprised. I glanced at Nathan and took a deep breath.

"Why me? Why you even? I mean, why are we cursed too?"

She hesitated. "I wondered the same things, except for me, there was nobody to ask. I don't know. Really, I don't. I sometimes wonder if I had an ancestral werewolf. I believe that was more common in the old days. But we've never taken part in any kind of genetic testing, so we'll never know for sure if it's a trait that's been passed down or if there's something bigger going on."

She left us with that enigmatic thought. I rubbed my forehead. "I've never felt so confused in my life."

Nathan and I strolled toward my house, neither of us saying it but both knowing we needed a bit of space. I couldn't help glancing around to see if anyone was there, but it was a nice day. There was no chill in the air. No feeling that unseen eyes were watching.

Nathan held my hand and, for a while, I felt almost normal.

"Do you ever see your mother?" he asked, out of the blue.

"No." I was so startled by the question, I forgot to avoid it.

"How come?"

"I don't want to. She doesn't want to. It all works out." I tried not to grip his hand a little tighter.

"You really don't?" His gaze was steady.

I let go of his hand and walked a little faster. "Look, I'm sorry about your mother. I know you probably don't want to talk about it, but I'm guessing she actually cared about you. Mine didn't. She didn't want to be a mother. She still doesn't. She probably never will."

He slipped his arm around my waist. "You never mention her."

"There's nothing to say. I mean, I don't even know her. She ran off when I was a baby. She didn't even tell anyone she was planning to leave. She saw me a couple of times when I was younger. She sends me things, just to make her conscience a bit easier to take or something. I have a family, and she isn't part of it."

"Would you like to know her?" he said, his voice softening.

I bit my lip, unsure of how to answer. I always acted as if I didn't want her around, but sometimes I wondered what it would be like. "I don't know. I think I'd feel like I was betraying my Dad or something. I mean, she did a really bad thing to him. If I was suddenly her best pal, it would be like I forgave her for what she did. Like it would make it okay? Does that make sense?"

"Totally. But, sometimes, you have to keep your feelings separate from your Dad's. She might have messed things up, but that doesn't mean you have to keep punishing her either."

"Really? I don't know. She's still being a nuisance without even seeing her, so imagine how bad things could be if she was around. At least now I know how I feel. If I started seeing her, she might disappoint me."

"How is she a nuisance now?"

"It's complicated. Dad and Gran are odd with each other, and it's mostly because of her. They're never totally comfortable together, and all of their rows stem from her in some way." I shrugged. He didn't speak, and I felt like the words were spilling out of me, so I carried on. "Gran wants me to be, like, the second edition of my mother, only better. The one who never leaves. Dad wants me to be the opposite of my mother. He and Gran argue about everything.

Gran wants me to use the things my mother sends, while Dad wants me to bin them. It's gotten better lately, but still, every bad thing that happens seems to come from her."

It was hard to admit how I really felt but, for the first time in my life, I was able to talk about her without choking up. Nathan was a good listener, and it just seemed right to tell him things. At least the curse made *some* things easier.

***

That week, Dad decided it was time for Gran and me to get to know Erin a little better. First, he brought her over for dinner, and when that didn't end in disaster, she started coming over in the evenings when he wasn't at work—just to hang out.

Erin was okay. I barely knew her, so I wasn't altogether comfortable in her company, but she seemed pleasant, and she looked at my Dad in a way that endeared her to me. Although it was strange that Dad had a girlfriend, I was happy as long she didn't hurt him.

Gran was another story. She wasn't openly rude, but I saw her face grow tighter and tighter each evening, as if she was holding in what she really wanted to say. I hoped she kept on holding it in, because I didn't want to hear it.

Chapter Fourteen

Tammie waited impatiently for my tutoring session with Joey to be over. She sighed incessantly, distracting me, but I was already having trouble concentrating. Werewolves and gypsy curses took a lot of mulling over.

I slammed my book shut. "Any chance we can finish up early today?"

"How come?" Joey looked relieved.

"Nathan's coming over soon. We're going to tell Dad about me and him."

"So it's true then," Tammie said, sounding harsh. "You're really with him now."

I nodded, tired of talking to her.

"Didn't take you long to worm your way into that one. Don't come crying to me when he breaks your heart."

"Don't worry, Tammie. You're the last person I'll ever run to for help." I shook with anger, unable to understand where my friend had gone.

"It's okay, Perdy," Joey said, ignoring Tammie. "I know you like him, so he's cool with me."

I grinned at Joey, grateful I could rely on him. I was beginning to think I underestimated him a lot.

"What if *I* don't want him around?" Tammie pouted.

"Tough for you then, isn't it?" he said without missing a beat.

Tammie looked as though she was going to fall off her chair. I almost swelled with pride. Joey didn't make a habit of getting involved when Tammie decided to be bitchy but, when he did, he really put her in her place. She wasn't happy, but she kept quiet until they left. Yet again, I was left wondering why things had changed so much between us all.

Nathan called around soon after—I was even more nervous than I expected, but I had to bite the bullet if I wanted to spend more time with him. I just hoped Dad would be reasonable.

"Dad, you remember Nathan, right?"

"I'm not senile, Perdy. Hi again, Nathan." Dad beamed at Nathan.

I took a deep breath. "So. Nathan and I are sort of seeing it each other now. Kind of."

"Like a couple," Nathan clarified. I winced, unsure of how Dad would take that description. The smile fell from his face, but Erin was in the room. He couldn't act like himself without coming across badly to his girlfriend, so he was forced to suck it up and deal with it. By the time Erin left, I hoped he would have calmed down.

"Oh. Right. Well. That's nice," he said, his speech stilted. But he leaned toward Nathan and whispered in his ear. "I know where you live."

Gran rolled her eyes. "Stephen! Don't mind him, Nathan. Sit next to me."

Nathan winked at me and let Gran lead him into the living room.

"This is new," Dad said with a frown.

"Yup." I couldn't think of anything else to say.

"Well," he said, glancing at Erin. "Be careful then."

"Um, okay." Awkward.

Erin draped her arm around my shoulder. "Let's go rescue your *boyfriend* from Ruth." She giggled at the look on Dad's face, and I got the impression she was really rescuing *me* from Dad.

Gran spent at least an hour embarrassing me and making fun of Dad's discomfort. Dad did better than I expected though, and I could only thank Erin for that.

"Anyone want a drink?" she asked, getting to her feet.

"Coffee, please," Dad said, somehow managing to make the words sound affectionate. Erin turned to Gran and smiled expectantly. Gran stared at Erin with a strange expression on her face. She turned to me, ignoring Erin.

"Oh, Perdy, I almost forgot. Your mother rang earlier, looking for you."

Dad's head snapped toward Gran, his eyes narrowing. Erin froze on the spot, unsure of herself. I shrugged at Gran, once again feeling like I was being thrown into the middle of something.

"Don't you think you should ring her back?" Gran persisted with the game she was playing.

"No, actually."

"Maybe you could invite her to stay for a weekend or something."

I couldn't believe what I was hearing. "She didn't want to be here when it was her home. It's not hers anymore, so why would she want to be here now?" I stood, ignoring my Gran's face. "Think I'll help you with that coffee, Erin."

Erin followed me into the kitchen. We didn't speak, but she squeezed my hand briefly as she passed me by to switch on the kettle. Gran seemed intent on marking her territory in the house, but Erin took it in her stride. She didn't give Gran any ammunition, and I found I was becoming fond of her.

Gran did accomplish something. The nice, calm atmosphere vanished completely. Later, I tried to ease Gran into the idea of Erin being a permanent fixture.

"Erin's lovely," I said. "I really like her, and Dad seems to be smitten. Think she's gonna move in?"

Gran looked so horrified that I knew I had made a mistake. "Of course not. This is your *mother's* house."

"No. It isn't. You have to stop thinking that way," I said, trying to be gentle. "It hasn't been her house for a very long time."

"Well, it's my house then. Nobody's moving in here." She crossed her arms stubbornly, looking like a spoiled child.

"What if Dad moves out?" I felt exasperated by her.

"Don't be silly. He'll never leave you." She went upstairs in a huff before I could tell her he could take me with him. I really hoped Gran wouldn't make life difficult for Erin.

When Nathan had to go, I walked him outside.

"I'm sorry," he said. "The almighty Byron decided there are no werewolves here anymore, so there's nothing to worry about. If anything happens, and I mean, *anything*, then just call me. Okay?"

I agreed, but I hoped I wouldn't have to.

"I have a favour to ask, too. I'm not going to school tomorrow, because Mémère is insisting we all go hunting while Amelia is surrounded by people. We should be back by the time Amelia gets home but, just in case we aren't, could you bring her here after school?"

"Of course. Hunting, eh? Is that what you were doing the time Amelia said you were in the cinema, and you said you were visiting old friends?" I laughed at his face.

"Get you, Nancy Drew. Yeah, probably. We haven't exactly coordinated our lies." He grinned and kissed me until I couldn't remember what I was going to say next.

***

"I'm sooo glad to be outside again," Amelia said, stretching her arms. "You'd think I had some kind of plague and not a cold, the way my family carried on."

"At least you got a few days off school. I'm just going to run to my locker. See you in the lunchroom."

I threw my bag into my locker and headed back, but as I passed by an empty classroom, I saw Joey sitting alone, eating his lunch.

"Um, what are you doing in here?" I said.

He jumped about a foot in the air, his neck and face turning bright red. "I'm…" He spluttered to a stop. "Okay, I'm avoiding Tammie."

I took a seat. "Avoiding her? How come?"

He stared at his lunch. "This was a mistake, Perdy. She's acting crazy. I don't know what I was thinking getting involved. She was cool when we were friends, but now she's off her head."

"Did she do something in particular?" I tried to feel bad for Tammie, but she had been acting crazy around me too.

"It's just a constant stream of questions and texts and calls. She wants to know *everything*. And she seems to hate anyone else in the world being happy. I don't get her. She just makes me tired. I feel like she's draining me."

"Wow, I'm sorry. I don't really know what to say. Maybe it'll all blow over in a few days."

"I hope so. You go on. I'm going to get some studying done. That's my excuse anyway." He smiled weakly. I left him, feeling really helpless. Maybe Gran had been right about not getting involved after all.

At lunch, Tammie was predictably sour, but I ignored that as much as possible and acted as though the last few weeks hadn't happened.

After school, I tried to persuade Amelia to come to my house, but she refused.

"I know what he said." She folded her arms stubbornly. "But King's at home alone. You can come with me if you like, but I'm going home."

I gave up after a while; she was determined to go to her own house. Exasperated, I joined her and hoped the rest of her family had already returned. I was trying so hard not to think of Nathan eating defenceless animals—raw—that I didn't have the energy to keep arguing with Amelia.

When we got to her house, something bugged me, but I couldn't figure out what. As she fiddled with the key, I realised what it was—no dog running out to greet us. Any time I had been at the house, either King or Cúchulainn had been the first to welcome me.

I followed Amelia inside and bumped into her when she skidded to a stop. Her face paled, and she pointed ahead. The floor was covered in drops of blood.

"King?" she called, sounding scared and unsure. I backed out, pulling her after me and heard a vicious growl as I swiftly slammed the door behind us. Something crashed against it, scaring the hell out of me.

"We have to go. Hurry!" I shouted at her, but she wouldn't run. "Come on, Amelia!"

"But King... was that King?"

I pulled her arm and urged her on. "No, it wasn't King. Drop your bag and run. Faster. There's no time to explain everything. There are werewolves after me."

"It's okay. We shut the door," she said, dumbly.

"Newsflash! Werewolf! Can turn into a man and open the poxy door!"

She seemed to get a grip then and ran even faster than me. I fished my mobile out of my pocket and rang Nathan's phone, getting his voicemail. I huffed out a shaky message.

"Nathan! Something's happened. We're running to my place; they were in your house. I think they... Amelia, no!" I dropped the phone in my haste. Amelia ran away from me, toward the woods.

"Shortcut!" she shouted.

"No, stay on the path. Amelia! Stop!"

I swore as she ran straight into the trees. I glanced around, didn't see any wolves—not that I expected them to run down the road in full view—and followed her, hoping they would leave us alone.

Chapter Fifteen

I ran through the trees, ignoring the goose bumps on my arms and the hair rising on the back of my neck. I could barely see a thing in the thick patch of trees. Why on earth had Amelia chosen the woods to hide in? I tried to run but kept tripping up over rocks and roots.

Panting, I called Amelia but heard no reply. My heart pounded; things were spiralling out of control. I thought the werewolves were after me, so why had they been in Amelia's home—waiting for her?

A scream startled me. I wasn't sure where it came from, but I heard another, and this time the sound was clear enough for me to get a general direction. I ran as fast as I could until I found Amelia.

A huge reddish brown wolf prowled in front of her, growling and snarling as it stalked her. I looked around for something to hit it with but only saw a piece of rock that wasn't very heavy. Without thinking, I hurled it at the wolf with every bit of strength I had in me. It hit the animal in the side. The wolf yelped, more from surprise than pain, and sprang around to face me instead.

"Run, Amelia!" I screamed.

She hesitated then sprinted away. The wolf was terrifying. Its eyes were yellow and wild, and its snarl, inhuman. I gulped with apprehension as it approached me. It sniffed the air eagerly. I knew it could sense my fear.

I stepped backward slowly as the wolf leaned low, ready to spring. Tripping, I fell awkwardly. The wolf lurched forward, its lips curled back to reveal huge sharp teeth. I squeezed my eyes shut, too scared to watch. I tensed up, but nothing happened. I opened one eye cautiously, only to see the wolf feint another attack. He was taunting me. I gulped, too frozen with fear to move or even scream. I was sure I was about to die as I looked into those wild amber eyes.

I recognised them and knew for sure it was the red-haired man; werewolves had been following us all along. They knew the truth about us way before I did. But how?

"You," I gasped, unable to help myself. "Why are you doing this?"

He cocked his head to the side. An intense shudder ran through his entire body.

For a second I thought he was going to let me live, but then he crouched, about to launch himself at me, and the world slowed down. A huge black blur flung itself at the red wolf. He rolled over, shaking himself free, and leapt to his feet. He looked from me to the black wolf, hesitating before running away.

The black blur looked around at me with the most beautiful brown eyes I had ever seen. His black coat shone with health. There was nothing scary in his expression, and I felt a pang of something inside.

"Nathan?" I whispered, in complete awe of him. I moved slowly toward him with my hand out. "You're beautiful."

I managed to lightly touch his coat with my fingers before he ran off. Being near him worked, we were going to be okay. Snapping out of the trance I had fallen into, I scrambled to my feet and hurried in the direction Amelia had headed toward, calling her name as loud as I dared. She scared the life out of me by grabbing my hand from behind a tree.

"Oh, my God! You're okay."

"Yeah, Nathan's here."

Her eyes darted about wildly. Her face was slick with sweat; her hair stuck to her face. She grabbed my arm, her fingertips pinching me in her urgency. She gulped repeatedly, unable to fully catch her breath. I had to stop her hyperventilating. I had to get us out of the woods.

I held her face still and forced her to look at me. "Listen to me. Just listen. We're going to be okay. Everything's going to be okay. I'm here. I'll take care of you. But I need you to calm down for me."

I held her close to me and shushed her until her breathing became almost regular again.

"No talking now, Amelia," I warned when I finally stopped her sobbing. "Listen to me. We have to get out of here as quietly as possible. We're going to head to my house. We'll be safe there. Do you understand? There are lots of people; it's public. They won't come after us." I had no idea if we'd be safe there. I knew she was in danger—I was too—but we had to keep moving no matter what.

Her entire body shook visibly. If she could only ground herself, she might keep it together long enough to make it to safety. I was determined not to let my own doubts show.

"Concentrate on getting out of here. Don't think about werewolves. Just watch your step." She gulped a couple of times and nodded, focusing.

She was terrified. I had never seen her look so young. I wasn't sure what was going on, but I knew we had to get ourselves out of the middle of it. I held her arm tightly and led her slowly onward. I had a rough idea of where we were, and I knew the area better than Amelia, but it was easy to get turned around when you were being chased by a mythical creature. Amelia had turned into a blubbering mess, so I had to take control and not think about the red wolf—or anything else that might be in the woods.

I concentrated on moving, one step at a time, keeping Amelia with me. I felt stronger for looking after her, but rivulets of sweat ran down my back nonetheless. I couldn't let myself lose it when I had to make sure she was safe. One thought in my mind kept me going. Nathan. Before he came along, I would have probably lost the plot just like Amelia, but now he was my strength. I pushed on because of him, for him.

We ran as fast as we could, but exposed tree roots, growing darkness, and complete panic slowed us down. After what seemed like an eternity, I realised we had to be close to the edge of the woods. Just when I thought we would be okay, a nasty snarl from behind us proved we clearly weren't. We were in a much less dense area of the woods, so it was easy to see that two growling wolves were behind us, closing in.

One was almost blonde in colour with ice blue eyes that were as cold as they were ferocious. I guessed it was the angry blonde woman. But it was the bigger wolf who really scared me. I could see him more clearly this time. Mostly grey with dark streaks of black, he looked completely feral. His mouth curled back in an aggressive snarl, saliva and foam dripping down his chin. I knew he was a werewolf, but he didn't seem like he could be human at all.

Nathan's eyes had remained soft when he changed, but this wolf had manic eyes. He moved toward us, inching ahead of the other wolf. I could see his focus was on Amelia, so I pushed her behind me hoping to distract him. She clung to the back of my jacket, terrified.

The wolf paused and looked at me, sniffing the air. He lifted his head and barked harshly, still heading straight for us. The blonde wolf lined up beside him, soon joined by the third wolf. I backed up, not sure what to do next. I knew they would kill us just as surely as I knew they were all werewolves.

I was wondering how far we could run before being caught when two black wolves burst through the trees, snarling in anger. Amelia gave a little shriek of alarm. I grabbed her arm and forced her backward. I recognised Nathan and assumed the larger, shaggier one was Byron. I hadn't gotten a good look at him before. Now I saw he was fierce and magnificent, but not as beautiful as Nathan in wolf form.

The blonde and red wolves both turned to face Nathan and Byron automatically, but the grey one ignored them and continued to focus on us—more specifically, Amelia. He barely looked around when two more wolves and some wolfhounds joined the scene. It wasn't until they surrounded him, snapping and snarling that he turned his body away from us. I swallowed a scream. He still seemed reluctant to lose sight of Amelia.

I wasn't sure if there were more werewolves around, so I was afraid to run. I'd heard that running entices an animal's hunting instinct, but I had no idea if that still applied. I didn't have a clue what to do. Life hadn't exactly prepared me for killer werewolves.

I already knew the large white wolf was Jakob Evans, and I guessed the smaller silvery grey wolf was Lia. They weren't as intimidating as Byron, but they stood their ground. The wolfhounds backed off as one, as if they had been commanded. They surrounded Amelia and myself. Amelia clung to Cúchulainn, sobbing loudly. I was afraid she was drawing attention to herself. The wild looking grey wolf was obviously distracted by the sounds she made; his body shuddered every time she let out a sob. I gripped her shoulder tightly, silently urging her to calm down.

All of the werewolves faced each other for a few tense moments. I was terrified for Nathan. He was the least experienced wolf being so young. As far as I could tell, an immature werewolf had no chance against a full grown, experienced werewolf.

My blood ran cold at the thoughts of him fighting against an adult wolf. For the first time, it truly dawned on me how much danger we were all in. Although his family outnumbered the others, they weren't used to these kinds of confrontations. The other werewolves gave me the impression they had done this before. Particularly when they snarled and snapped threateningly.

For one tense moment, nobody made a move. The grey wolf's body trembled constantly, as if he was trying to restrain himself. He seemed more than eager to fight. As if one, all three of the wolves unknown to me attacked.

The large grey one went straight for Lia. He had her throat before Jakob could respond. She fought back fiercely, squirming to get away, her nostrils flaring. Jakob jumped onto the wolf's back, forcing him to let go. The three of them rolled around together. It was immediately obvious the elderly couple were no match for the younger, stronger, wilder wolf.

Byron seemed to be getting the upper hand on the red wolf, but I was distracted by something else. The blonde wolf had thrown herself at Nathan who rolled backward and struck his head off a tree stump. For a moment he lay there, stunned and motionless. Those few seconds felt like an eternity to me. The wolf took advantage and attacked him, sinking her teeth into his neck, to my horror. I glanced back at the others and saw the grey wolf had gripped Lia in a similar way. Blood spurted onto his face. I had to make a choice.

Something inside me unleashed itself. As though a switch flipped, I thought of Nathan as my mate; I couldn't let anything happen to him. I didn't think about what to do next. I simply reacted.

I ran straight over to the blonde wolf, half climbing onto her back. I reached around and sank my fingers into her eyes with one hand, using the other to tear at her coat relentlessly, desperate to pull her away. One lone focus in my mind—to help Nathan. She yelped loudly in pain as I pulled at her, letting go of Nathan abruptly. I fell backward, pulling her after me with a burst of adrenalin that gave me strength I never had before.

She landed heavily on top of me, almost crushing me with her weight. I was sure I heard one of my ribs crack, but I didn't let go of her fur. She growled in my ear and struggled to twist her body around. I moaned in pain from her weight as she shifted herself in preparation to destroy me. I flinched in anticipation, but Nathan recovered in time. He sank his jaws around her flank and pulled her from me, apparently unable to control his fury. She snapped at empty air instead of my throat.

Seeing her hurt me had changed something inside of Nathan too, I could tell. He was freeing his mind of all human thought. I could sense his rage and felt a strange sort of pride as he snarled even more ferociously than her. I knew with certainty he wouldn't let her near me again. He was fierce and wild, and I realised I had to get out of the way, because he was letting his animal instincts take over.

I scrambled to my feet, side-stepping out of the way as they both tumbled toward me again. Gasping with pain, I ran back to the wolfhounds who were howling with disapproval. They had been commanded to stay with Amelia, but they wanted to protect me, too.

Amelia's face was stained from a mixture of black eyeliner and steady tears. I ignored her, irrationally angry at her weakness. I touched Cúchulainn on the head reassuringly; he was the one most agitated by the fight. He licked my hand and tried to nudge me back toward Amelia, but I was too busy looking for a large stick I could pick up.

A sharp pain in my side almost doubled me over when I lifted a branch, but I ignored it as best I could. Both Nathan and Byron were covered in blood, but I was pretty sure most of it wasn't theirs. The blonde wolf in particular was panting heavily, her coat matted dark red in places.

It was Lia and Jakob whom I worried about the most. The big grey wolf was strong, stronger than any of the others, and he had done something bad to Lia Evans while I had been trying to help Nathan. She lay on the ground, curled up in a ball, taking shallow breaths that somehow sounded wet. A sickening amount of blood flowed freely from an open wound at the base of her throat.

The grey werewolf crouched over Jakob Evans. His jaws wrapped around Jakob's neck in a death grip as he shook him violently. I could almost see the life leave Jakob. He was growing weaker by the second, his struggles lessening too quickly. I realised it was probably too late for Lia, but I was determined to help Jakob.

The grey werewolf was so busy savaging Jakob that he didn't notice me approach him from behind. I lifted the branch as high as I could, almost passing out with the pain. I slammed it down hard on the grey wolf's head. He grunted, but held on, unable to take himself away from a kill. I struggled to lift the branch again, gasping from the intense pain in my ribs. This time I pounded it down harder, the impact making a sickening thud.

He released Jakob immediately and let out a horrible cry. He turned and looked right at me, blood dripping from his snout. I dropped the branch, unable to look away. A shadow darkened his eyes, and he fell to the ground. Lifeless. I froze, waiting for him to get back up.

He didn't.

Both of his companions immediately raised their heads in our direction at the sounds. The blonde one whimpered, but the other barked and they both fled in unison, Nathan snapping at the blonde's tail.

Jakob limped up with difficulty and nosed Lia on the ground. I held my breath, but she didn't stir. I shook my head in disbelief. Not Lia. It couldn't be possible. Tears rolled down my eyes at the heart-breaking sound of Jakob's mournful howl. He leapt up and chased after the two escaping wolves, followed by Byron and some of the wolfhounds. A snarl from Byron forced Nathan back toward us.

In the back of my head, I could hear Amelia screaming, but it was dull, as if there was something muffling my ears. Nathan sniffed his grandmother's face and let out an awful howl that made me choke back a sob. I couldn't just stand there, or I'd fall apart completely. I had to do something. I hated the thoughts of Lia being so close to the monster that killed her, so I struggled to pull him away by his back legs. It took me ages, and it hurt like hell, but I had to do something.

Nathan lay next to Lia. I wondered if her body would return to its normal shape. I was still struggling with the grey wolf's body when Byron and Jakob returned to us in their human forms, barefooted and bare-chested, along with the other wolfhounds. I vaguely wondered where their trousers had come from. When Byron saw what I was trying to do, he helped, lifting the dead werewolf easily and carelessly throwing him as far away from his mother as he could manage.

Byron and Jakob knelt beside Nathan. Amelia crawled over to join them. Nathan shook almost as much as Amelia. I hung back, not wanting to intrude on their grief. Jakob was in bad shape; he had deep wounds on his body, and Byron was covered in cuts and scratches. It was too hard to tell how badly hurt Nathan was, but I prayed he would be okay.

Lia would never be okay, and neither would Jakob; he lost his soul mate. He had to be heartbroken. I couldn't begin to imagine what that felt like. Even I would miss Lia's warm, comforting presence. I hadn't known her for long, but she helped me. She had believed me. Even wanted to protect me. I owed her. It wasn't fair she was gone. She didn't deserve to die. If I had only helped her. If I hadn't needed help. No matter how I looked at it, the blame fell on my shoulders.

I sat down beside Cúchulainn because I didn't know what else to do. I looked down at myself and saw my clothes were now covered in dark red blood. None of it mine. The realisation of what happened hit me abruptly. I had just killed someone. As the thought connected in my brain, my body began to shudder violently. He died, right in front of me. The animal who would turn back into a man.

Even though he was shaped like a wolf, he was human. I killed a man. Me. A murderer. Only sixteen years old, and I had the deaths of two people on my conscience. Lia, and the werewolf who killed her. Cúchulainn licked my face, but I was too freaked out to respond. I had watched the light go out in the werewolf's eyes, and I had been glad of it. What kind of a monster did that make me?

"She's gone into shock."

I didn't know who was talking until Byron lifted me to my feet. I was too out of it to feel surprised when he hugged me tightly.

"I saw what you did. It's going to be okay. You had no choice."

I tried to speak, but my throat closed up completely. Not that I could say anything that would make any of it better. I wanted to lie down and not get up again. I didn't understand why everything had gone so wrong.

Byron lifted his mother carefully and respectfully, his father close by his side. Seeing her body in his arms made it sink in, and I wasn't able to stop the tears from falling. I choked back a loud sob, telling myself I didn't have a right to cry. I felt incredibly out of place and alone.

I was suddenly aware of Amelia's hand squeezing mine, and Nathan's animal form pushing against my other hand. I gripped his fur tightly and felt stronger for it. Amelia leaned against me, but I took comfort from the touch. We all left the woods together, covered in blood and united in grief. I followed Byron, sandwiched between my best friend and my boyfriend. Linked to each other in a brand new way.

Chapter Sixteen

We made it to their house without seeing anybody. I was grateful because it would have been too much to explain. Despite the risk of being seen, neither Jakob nor Byron appeared to worry. Keeping secrets just didn't seem important anymore.

Our procession moved slowly. Even Nathan didn't seem to care about being seen in his wolf form.

At the house, I waited in the sitting room alone while the others brought Lia's body up to her bedroom. I felt like an intruder in their home. I sat there, covered in blood that wasn't my own, and wept. So many regrets spun around in my mind. I didn't know where to start processing what had actually happened. I wasn't even close to wondering how I could explain it all to my father. Byron joined me, throwing a jumper over his head. He ignored my tears.

"Let me see your ribs," he commanded. He pressed gently against them until I winced, then he wrapped a bandage around my torso. "This will have to do for now. I'm going to get rid of… the body in the woods. Stay here until I get back. We need to talk. My father is performing a death ritual upstairs, so sit here quietly, all right?"

I nodded glumly, not bothering to ask how he was getting rid of the body or what a death ritual entailed. I couldn't take any more information. He left me alone again. All I could think about was poor Lia Evans, and how I hadn't helped her in time.

Nathan came to find me after he had showered the grime and blood from his body. I lifted his top and checked him carefully, more relieved than I could say when I saw how little he had been hurt. He let me, as if knowing I would break down completely unless I saw for myself.

"Amelia's with King." Nathan shook his head. "They hurt him bad. He didn't make it."

"I'm sorry. I'm so sorry," I spluttered, unable to say anything else. He held on to me, his presence so reassuring that I almost calmed down. I felt so bad, so guilty, so sure I had caused it all. I couldn't take it back. No matter how much I wanted to.

"I'm sorry," I said again. He pulled back and looked me in the eye, seeing everything I couldn't say. He kissed me fiercely, our bodies entwined as if we would never let go. I thought he would blame me. I thought he might even hate me for letting the whole thing begin. And worse, for missing the chance to help his grandmother. I thought a lot of things, but they all faded away when he held me.

"I was so afraid for you. *So* afraid," he whispered in my ear. "Don't ever attack a werewolf again, please."

I almost laughed. "I won't, if you won't." He kissed my tears away. That only made more fall. "I'm so sorry I didn't help her in time," I said, my voice shaking. I couldn't say Lia's name. I was afraid to look at him, but he forced me to.

"What are you talking about? You helped me, you kept Amelia safe, and you saved my grandfather's life. You could have been killed, Perdita. Do you understand that? *We* brought this with us, and *you* could have been the one who got hurt." He stroked my cheek gently, and somehow it unleashed everything I was feeling.

"I killed him. I watched him die. And I wasn't sorry, Nathan. I wasn't sorry." I gasped for air as my stomach clenched so tight it felt as if I had been punched in the gut. I doubled over with pain, struggling to breathe—my ribs weren't the only cause. I kept seeing the wolf's, no, the man's eyes as he died on the ground in front of me. I heard the noise he made over and over. I saw Lia's broken body, and suddenly I couldn't stand anymore. Grief overwhelmed me, threatening to suck me into a blackness I was almost willing to lose myself in.

Nathan helped me to the sofa, holding my hand, and whispering comforting words until I calmed down.

"Listen to me," he said firmly. "I know how you're feeling. Trust me, but you can't let the guilt take over. He was a monster who wanted you to die. And Amelia too. They were going to kill you both. The three of them have been stalking you for months, Perdita. It's not your fault; you did more than most people would have. He was a killer, remember? It's our fault, if anything. We should have dealt with them straight away. We shouldn't have hidden ourselves away. Don't take on this guilt. It isn't yours to own."

I sniffed a few times and looked up at his determined face. He had aged in the last few hours. Seeing him helped me. He found strength from somewhere and that made me stronger too.

"I mean it," he continued. "If we had learned from our own kind then none of this would have happened. We should have gone after them; you should never have been in danger. I won't let it happen again, I promise you. I'm never going to let you feel like this again. You can't feel guilty for protecting yourself. And my grandmother didn't die for nothing." Tears slid from his eyes then, and that was enough for me to gain control over my emotions. It was my turn to comfort him. He had lost a lot more than me.

We were still embracing each other when the others returned. Byron's face was pale but determined. Amelia sat close to me, her eyes bloodshot from crying. I put my arm around her, feeling her sink into my embrace. Jakob sat with his head in his hands. I couldn't bear to look at him.

"The body was gone by the time I got back," Byron said. Hope blossomed in my chest until I realised it only meant the other wolves had come back first. He was still dead.

I hiccupped. "I have to talk to my Dad, and go to the police."

Byron's attention snapped back to me. "What are you talking about? You can't talk to anyone about this!"

I stared up at him. "I *killed* someone. Someone is dead because of me. I can't just get away with that!"

"Didn't you hear me? *There is no body*. I forbid you to speak of this with anyone." His words rumbled over me until a trickle of sweat rolled down my back. Byron's black eyes scared me.

Nathan tensed up next to me. "You forbid her?"

"Yes!" Byron ran out of patience. "I have to protect this family. How am I supposed to explain to the world that werewolves exist? The world isn't ready for this, and one dead murderous werewolf isn't worth our time. She will not tell a soul!" His voice rose into a shout, and he paced in front of Nathan, Amelia and I for a few minutes, his face grim as he lost himself in his thoughts. Finally, he stopped and faced us.

"Tell me exactly what happened."

"It's my fault," I said. "I should never have let Amelia come home."

"Stop it!" she cried. "It's not your fault. We came in and saw blood on the carpet. Perdita pushed me outside and slammed the door. Made me run. I panicked and went through the woods because it's quicker. I didn't think. I didn't know to be scared!"

Nathan turned to us. "We were on our way. We must have just missed you. We were trying to figure out what happened to King when I realised I had a missed call from Perdita. I listened to the message, and we tried to get to you first."

"They've been following me all along," I said. "But they came here for Amelia."

"She's right." Jakob raised his head, surprising us with his sudden input. "He wanted Amelia dead. He was barely able to force himself away from her even when we surrounded him."

"Everyone get ready. We're leaving," Byron said.

"Leaving?" I said, shocked at the idea. How could they leave me? I looked at Nathan, my chin trembling. I felt as though I lost a piece of myself anytime he walked away from me. How could I cope if he was gone for good?

He gazed back at me, looking as frightened as I felt. He shook his head slightly then turned to Byron expectantly.

"Don't worry, you two." Byron smiled, but his eyes stayed cold. "We'll take care of you, Perdita. We're going to leave, but you'll come with us, of course. We'll hide and be safe. We'll make sure they don't track us down again."

I shook my head, not sure I was understanding him correctly. "I'm not going anywhere."

"You have to," Byron's voice was a lot softer than usual. "We have to keep you three safe. You're all connected together. They won't stop until they hurt at least one of you. And hurting one will hurt the others. You understand?"

This was wrong. All wrong. I couldn't leave my family. My mother had done that. I was meant to stay with them. I was sick of hiding from the world. Let the werewolves come for me. I was filled with enough hate and rage and sorrow not to care. I knew the connection between myself, Nathan, and Amelia was powerful, and maybe even dangerous, but it didn't feel right to run away with them.

"I understand, but I don't agree. I'm not running, Byron. I'm not going to hide away for the rest of my life. If they come for me, well, I'll have to deal with it then, but I'm not abandoning my family to save myself. No way."

Nathan held my hand, supporting my decision in silence. Amelia leaned closer to me, clutching my arm.

"You don't have a choice, Perdita." Byron was annoyingly dismissive of everything what I wanted.

"Yes, she does," Nathan said, his voice firm. "And so do I. I'm not leaving her."

Byron gazed at him in concern but was even more surprised when his own father put his hand on his shoulder.

"They're right, son. We've hidden away for long enough. Let them come. We'll be ready next time. Hiding ourselves has been a mistake. I'm going to find out who they are and what they want. Then I'm going to deal with them. I won't lose any more of my family. They won't get away with it." The look on his face scared me. It was harsh and cold, everything Jakob wasn't. He wanted revenge. I didn't blame him.

"But, Dad." Byron sounded a little like me.

"I mean it, we're staying."

"I don't think…."

"Byron. We're *staying*."

Jakob's voice was surprisingly firm. Both men stared each other down.

"Stop it," Byron said, his voice less controlled.

"Stop what?" The tone of Jakob's voice was so cold, I couldn't stop shuddering.

"I'm the alpha. Stop trying to force your will on me! I can feel it," Byron shouted, panic in his eyes.

Nathan's hand tightened on mine, I wasn't sure what was happening, but it seemed important.

"We're staying," Jakob said, rock steady.

Amelia whimpered, but I watched, fascinated, as Byron finally bowed his head and turned away.

I could see the mix of emotion in Byron's conflicted expression and knew that I had won for now. He couldn't make me leave. Although he let it go, I was sure he would try again, even though Jakob was determined to stay.

It didn't matter because I knew I had Amelia, and more importantly, Nathan by my side. My life began to change when he came along, and now I knew I was a stronger person for it. We were cursed. All three of us.

Except now we had the truth on our side. The werewolves might leave us alone, but we had no way of knowing for sure. They didn't want us together; they probably wanted me dead. Living meant I would forever carry the heavy weight of the worst secrets. My Dad spent his life protecting me, and I had thrown it all away with one bad decision.

Byron banned me from telling anyone what I'd done; I was too scared of him to try his patience. But as long as Nathan was with me, I could carry on and fake being the same person I was before. The werewolves didn't want us together, but I was determined; I *needed* Nathan now. Nobody was going to separate us. I pitied anyone who wanted to try.

"Calm down! There's nothing we can do right now. I know you're upset, but getting yourself killed accomplishes nothing. We still have work to do." Ryan held Willow's arms tightly, expecting her to bolt again.

"I have to do something. You saw what she did to my father! The little coward, attacking us both from behind." Willow shook in anger, her face twisting into something ugly.

Deep down, Ryan pitied her, but he couldn't let her risk his life or his position in the pack. As if she knew what he was thinking, she sneered, looking him straight in the eye. Her height had always irritated him.

"Jack was careless. And so were you. She's just a human. We wasted our chance, and now we have to face the consequences. You know the rules," Ryan said, his voice low and careful.

She struggled against him, kicking out in her frustration. Only a hard slap across the face calmed her down. A trickle of blood ran from the corner of her mouth. She licked it slowly, all the while staring at him.

"Don't ever, *ever*, talk about my father. You're practically human yourself. You don't even come close to comparing to the wolf he is. The wolf he was. This isn't over. No matter what you say. Vin will agree, and then we'll see. I'll *never* let this day go. And when I'm done with them, I'll come after you. You'll see what my father taught me."

Her tone chilled him. He shivered in spite of himself at the hatred in her eyes. Her rank was less than his, and yet something about her terrified him. He was too weary to fight her; nothing had gone right. Both girls lived, the one werewolf female who had ever successfully bred healthy shifters was dead, and the alpha's prized fighter had been killed by a human teenager. It was a disaster.

He had nothing to worry about; Vin would kill him before Willow could even try. Ryan let her go, shaking his head. Willow stayed against the wall, hunched over slightly, her blonde hair covering most of her still blood-stained face. She seemed almost feral, ready to leap at him if he gave her an excuse.

"Willow. It wasn't my fault. It was his idea. I wanted to wait. Pick them off one by one. But you're right." He tried to placate her knowing he needed her story to back him up. "A cowardly attack killed your father. A fluke. He was unlucky. She'll pay for it, but first we need to let the others know what happened. If we stick together, we'll be okay." He brushed the hair back from her face carefully, hearing a low whimper.

She sucked her lower lip and sank to the floor, holding her knees and rocking herself. Her eyes were black and wild, but she was shut off from the world, lost in her own mind. Ryan sank down next to her, his forehead creased with worry. He had seen Willow's 'episodes' before, leaving her be and waiting was his only choice. She had always been unstable, but now Jack was gone, it would be worse. He often wondered how badly damaged her mind really was. Mating didn't work for werewolves, so what made the Evans family so special? Now the one female they really needed was dead, and they might never know the truth for sure.

Willow whimpered again. He stared at her, sympathy mingled with repulsion. She was a poor excuse for a wolf, despite the boasts of her family. He wasn't sure how he could control her now she was so intent on revenge. But more importantly, he didn't know if the alpha would spare his life and give him another chance.

Ryan pulled out his wallet and stared longingly at the photo of his family. He had to do whatever it took to get them back. "I'm tired of this, Willow," he whispered to the unresponsive shifter, knowing she couldn't hear him. "I don't want to die. I don't want to kill. I sure as hell don't want to babysit a werewolf with mental problems. How did we mess up so bad? They'll never let me go home now."

He groaned, frustrated. All they had achieved was giving the Evans family an excuse to want them dead. Things were going to get messy. He could only hope he survived the next fight.

About the Author

Claire Farrell is an Irish author and mother to five young children, including a set of twins. She enjoys infusing paranormal themes with a variety of genres, and all of her books are set in Ireland. When she isn't breaking up warring toddlers or inhaling coffee in order to stay awake, she likes to read, paint her nails purple, and listen to music. She welcomes correspondence from readers and can be reached through email, her blog, Facebook and even Twitter @DoingItWriteNow.

Acknowledgements

Thank you for reading and hopefully enjoying Verity – Book One of the Cursed series. A lot of things go into creating a story, and quite a few of them have nothing at all to do with the writer.

I would like to thank Periwinkle for making sure Verity wasn't released last year, way before it was ready. Seriously, thanks!

Also, to Verity's original online fans who loved the spark of the idea I had and encouraged me to finish the story. A special thanks to Verity's Wattpad fans; they somehow managed to see a diamond in the rough. The comments there ultimately made me publish Verity.

The biggest thanks must go to my very own soul mate. For being exactly who he is. Taking over as warring toddler separator helped too. ☺

And love to all five of my beautiful children for inspiring me to write books they might someday like to read.

About Verity

Verity is the first in a series of books. Book two of the Cursed series should be released in the spring of 2012. Expect repercussions, new characters, big reveals, and more from Nathan's point of view.

Many of the scenes in Verity were written while listening to musicians such as Oh Land, Amy Winehouse, Muse, Adele, KatyB, and Imelda May. If I had to pick one song, it would be Oh Land's 'Wolf and I'; it is beautiful.

.

Made in the USA
Lexington, KY
12 August 2012